The Great LAKESIDE HIGH Experiment

NEIL R. SELDEN

SCHOLASTIC INC.
New York Toronto London Auckland Sydney Tokyo

Cover Photo by Owen Brown

ISBN 0-590-31709-1

12 11 10 9 8 7 6 5 ·   5 6/8

Printed in the U.S.A.   06

The Great
LAKESIDE
HIGH
Experiment

A Wishing Star Book

One

Jen

First I'd better explain how the Love Experiment got started and how we picked Maude Harris as our guinea pig.

If someone had told me that during my senior year I would spend more time with Maude Harris than with any other single person, I'd have said, "You'd better go see a dentist, because you must have a cavity in your brains!"

But the Love Experiment was my idea, so I don't have any right to complain about what happened, even though it shook up a lot of people's lives, including mine.

The idea for the Love Experiment came to me on the day a wide-bodied 747 jet flew me back from Las Vegas. If you're ever annoyed with your boyfriend because he takes a full-time summer job instead of spending every minute with you on the beach, don't go off in a huff to visit your Aunt Wilma in Las Vegas. You can't imagine how bored you can get, in spite of the great hotels and star-studded shows, when Aunt Wilma practically Scotch-tapes herself to you, except when she sets you up with a bunch of boys and girls who are so straight you could use them for rulers.

I bounced off the 747, wearing a big beautiful fake smile, ready to entertain my friends with colorful anecdotes about a terrific summer that never happened, but of course not a single hello person was there to meet me, because I had written my mother *definitely not* to tell Larry when I was arriving and *not* to come herself. Knowing she'd tell Larry anyway, I was sure that he and our friends would pounce on me when I arrived. Airports are zilch when you're hurt and angry that nobody's there for you even though you set it up that way. Angry? I was furious!

Dozens of suitcases, none mine, went around and around on the moving rubber track. Next to me, a gray little apple dumpling lady smiled shyly. It was obvious she thought I was terrifically pretty, because I've seen a lot of people look at me that way. I wanted to explain to her why my dizzy frizzy blond hair, far-out makeup, and whole life had a kind of emptiness I couldn't understand, and that it didn't make sense because I had almost everything a girl could possibly want.

The suitcases went round and round, and so did the whole dumb senior year ahead of me at Lakeside High: the same old faces, talk, homework, jumping up and down like a nut with the other cheerleaders every time

Larry throws a pass, silly classes like Creative Sewing or Problems of World Hygiene, and worst of all this year, the endless talk about college applications. The gray-haired lady picked her suitcase off the moving track, wrinkling her eyes at me as if she wished we had spoken, and her face gave me a stab of sadness. I can't *stand* being sad. Jen, baby, get your act together!

Just when my suitcases appeared on the moving track, a pair of warm, rough hands closed over my eyes and somebody said, "Guess who?" It was Larry: half a smile on his broad, strong face; a dimple in the chin; eyes that crinkled; soft sandy hair; a slim, powerful body. He placed a casual kiss on my cheek, too casual.

"Hi, Larry!" I gave my voice a sprinkling of the usual Jen Robbins sunshine, hoping Larry wouldn't hear the lostness underneath, yet also hoping he would.

He said, "How was Las Vegas?"

I said, "Fabulous! How was your job at the animal lab?"

"Fabulous."

"I bet all the mice were crazy about you."

He fell silent, seeming for an instant unprotected and I almost spilled out my true feelings of loneliness, but suddenly two more guys came sailing over, Dolph Krager and Wayne Grants, hollering and clowning, and lifted me into the air.

"We're taking you out to Cold Springs River!" Wayne sang, his ever-present guitar strapped to his back; his hair long, dark, glossy, curly; his face very pale and almost too handsome.

Dolph, Larry's football teammate, blew me a kiss. He was a guy about 6' 4", all muscle, craggy nice looks, who never got rid of the dark shadow on his cheeks no matter what blades or shaving cream he tried.

Each of them hoisted one of my bags on top of his head and moved out single file, grunting loudly, like bearers in a safari.

Larry's battered pickup truck still had a broken muffler that sounded like a French horn with asthma, but the peeling blue paint, the rust holes, and the crack in the windshield were like marks on the face of an old friend.

My house was empty, as usual, when we got there; messy, as usual, and lonely, as usual. While Larry, Dolph, and Wayne were jacking up the truck to slap glob on a wheel bearing, I fitted myself into new knock-'em-dead jeans and then found a note from my mother. She said she had an emergency meeting of Strike Against Hunger and would see me later. My mom, always ready to put a Band-Aid or two on the poor bleeding world. I did notice she had added an expensive gold frame to a photo of Larry hugging me and hung it in the living room, which infuriated me because it felt like she was throwing me at him. It even made me angry at Larry that he was so perfect that my parents practically slobbered over him, so I yanked the picture off the wall.

That was where Maude Harris came in, and maybe the first glimmer of doing a Love Experiment on her. By pure accident, we zipped past her twice in the Five Star Food Mart where we were snapping items off the shelves for a cookout at Cold Springs River. Wayne and I were racing our shopping carts up and down the aisles; Larry and Dolph were flipping a football back and forth over the shelves. We saw Maude Harris the way you see a bag of potatoes, so *blah* she was almost invisible, but she must have registered on me because her image came back to me later: her dull brown hair in tight braids, shoulders slumping over her shopping cart, grim eyeglasses staring at the floor, and washed-out shapeless purple dress all wrong for her complexion.

Minutes later, Larry and I sat leg-to-leg in the cab of his noisy old pickup truck. Wayne and Dolph, bare-chested, soaking up sun in the open back of the truck, hung on for dear life whenever a pothole made the truck bed spring like a trampoline.

"Did you miss me?" Larry asked loudly.

My voice trembled. "I was too busy hanging around with Neil Diamond and Sinatra and all those stars in Las Vegas."

His voice softened. "I didn't miss you either."

"I want to thank you, Larry, for not calling me all summer. It was sweet of you to spare my sensitive eardrums."

In a husky tone that sent a lot of caring vibrations my way, he said, "And I'm glad you didn't write me any letters. All that reading would have damaged my eyesight."

Very quickly, very lightly, very briefly, we touched our lips together as if we were both admitting how dumb we had been.

"Friends?" Larry asked.

I traced my fingertips along the back of his neck and he shivered. "You date any guys this summer?"

"Dozens. You date any girls?"

"Hundreds."

Stopped at a railroad crossing, Larry pressed his mouth against mine, hard, but I pulled away.

"What's the matter, Jen?"

I winked one eye exaggeratedly at him to hide the sadness that had started nagging me again. "Las Vegas was so exciting I got hooked on it, and now I'm having the first phase of withdrawal symptoms."

"That's my girl, never forgets a phase!" he cracked.

I wished I couldn't fool him so easily. I wished he knew, without my telling him, what a mess of mixed-up emotions lay under my flashy Jen Robbins image. There was an ache in the center of me I couldn't even give a name to.

I leaned my head out the window. Warm September air whipped through the roots of my hair. I was trying hard to have a terrific time because the four of us — Larry, me, Dolph, Wayne — were coming together again after the entire summer apart. Dolph was yelling, "Whoopee! Ride 'em!" at every big bump of the truck; Wayne was smashing out chords of his newest song on the steel-string guitar. Sometimes it seemed we weren't complete without Dolph and Wayne, Larry's best friends, who had become sort of my best friends too, although I didn't really consider anyone, boy or girl, not even Larry, to be my *real* best friend, the kind of person you can tell *everything* to.

Even over the rumbling of the truck, the words of Wayne's new song grabbed at me, his voice really strong and a little harsh and hurting:

> We will never forget
> The games we played,
> We will never forget
> The plans we laid,
> The prayers we prayed,
> The price we paid
> For love.
> There was love
> But we didn't show it,
> There was love
> Though we didn't know it,
> There was love.

Mischievously, Larry shouted back into the wind, "Hey, Dolph, tell the Disco Kid back there he better score like Mt. Everest on the college entrance exams, because his songs are no competition for Barry Manilow!"

That was Larry's way of saying he loved the song. I reached my head and shoulders out the window as the ruts in the road shook the truck back and forth. "Wayne, don't listen to Larry! You know what kind of cologne he wears — it's called 'Baloney Number Five'!"

Seventeen miles from town the truck spun to a stop where the water in Cold Spring River ran dark and deep. Climbing out of the truck bed with a load of food, Dolph grinned at Wayne. "Pardner, do us a song about us three years hog-tied in that loco high school."

Dolph liked to imitate cowboys, even though he was originally from inner-city Boston before moving to Lakeside. He and Larry were the spark plugs of our football team, but they didn't make a big deal about it. His love life was one disaster after another, and I was always giving him emotional first aid. He kept falling for girls who were already ultra-involved with other guys.

As for Wayne, in his freshman year he wanted to be a songwriter-singer. His grades hit the cellar; he ran away to California, hitchhiking; he had a terrible time; he came back with his ribs sticking out. We were a lot alike: both of us very up all the time but secretly down on ourselves; both of us insane about outrageous new clothes, which Wayne could only afford by working after school in his father's belt factory and hating himself for doing it. I guess there was a little physical thing between Wayne and me, but we never said anything about it. Even if I wasn't exactly committed to Larry, I'd never get involved with a guy who was one of his best friends. Larry — Larry who seemed so intimate yet almost never talked about himself. Strange, I knew the least about Larry. Under all his joking, he was warm, strong, very kind; yet there was something I couldn't reach in him — like looking into dark water, something private, like the way his eyes would at odd times be so vulnerable, almost wounded.

Anyway, we found the circle of rocks from our last campfire months ago near the high old iron bridge, which connected the banks of Cold Spring River. The bridge was a relic of the days when freight cars chugged back and forth to the quarry where blocks of granite were torn out and hauled away. Now the quarry was our own private swimming pool when we got tired of the muddy river. First we swam in the dark, fast, cold river water and then we dived into the warm, glassy rainwater in the quarry. We toasted ourselves in the sun, joking and laughing, but I still had to work hard to keep my mind away from the ups and downs in my feelings about Larry. The whole sense of falseness bugged me, and I longed for something, I didn't know what. I had a sense of being about to lose something because our graduation, even though it was months and months away, would probably separate the four of us forever.

When the sun dropped behind a hill we quickly built our campfire, pulled on pants, socks, shirts. The sky darkened, flames grabbed at the first faint stars, frankfurters sizzled, and corn steamed. Larry began saying that we should somehow make our senior year something really special to remember, and not do the same old thing. I felt as if Larry was reading my mind, and I said that I agreed with him that we should do something different to show the whole system we were not just another bunch of machines off the assembly line.

None of us could think of any great idea to jazz up our senior year. Silence. Gloom. Depression. Wayne sang, which helped. Dolph told a cowboy story, which tickled us, and I earned a few laughs describing my Aunt Wilma. Then Larry told us details from his work that summer cleaning out the cages for the animal experiments and about how psychologists had demonstrated that monkeys who received no mother love grew up to be neurotic, unhappy loners. Some professors were now trying to see what effect love would have on mice — whether mice who were stroked, and caressed, and talked to affectionately by the experimenter would learn to run a maze faster than mice who were left alone.

That was when the idea for the Great Love Experiment popped into my mind, and the words tumbled out of me breathlessly.

"Suppose we tried an experiment like that with a human being in Lakeside High?"

"There *are* no human beings in Lakeside High, except us." Larry solemnly flung a chewed corncob into the fire.

"I'm serious, Larry! I bet nobody has tried an experiment like that with real people!" The idea excited me so much, suddenly my nagging sadness and the drifting little clouds of loneliness vanished.

"It's a wonderful chance for us to do someting *important!* Totally change someone's life! Say we pick out a real nowhere girl, a wallflower, and we act like her best friends, take her on double dates, treat her like she's great to be with, really *include* her. It could be fantastic for her."

Larry moaned. "You want us to spend our senior year dragging around some dumb girl?"

Wayne barged in. "An experiment like that could absolutely murder my reputation with women!"

"Before we bust our britches laughing," Dolph added, "who do you have in your noggin for the guinea pig?"

The boys laughed, but I was determined. Okay, what girl *could* I pick to be the guinea pig?

Maude Harris. Maude Harris pushing a shopping cart in the supermarket with her dull brown hair, tight braids, grim eyeglasses, and shapeless purple dress.

"Maude Harris!" I announced victoriously.

"Maude *Harris*?" Wayne's voice jumped an octave.

"Maude Harris!" Dolph barked. "Woman, you got a bad case of Rocky Mountain brain fever!"

"But she's the perfect person for Larry's experiment!" I ranted. "Isn't she, Larry?"

"*My* experiment?" Larry's eyebrows shot up.

"You're the one who told us all about the mice and the monkeys, Larry," I reminded him.

"Ah don't mind a-dyin' with mah boots on," Dolph groaned, "but Maude Harris is a fate worse than death!"

"Be serious!" I jumped up facing the three of them. "Maude Harris has — she has possibilities. There's nothing *basically* wrong with her. I mean there's nothing wrong with her mouth, for example."

The boys gave me dead looks.

"Her eyes are probably nice," I tried.

Dolph rolled his eyes up into his head, Wayne spread his mouth a foot wide with his fingers, and Larry sucked his cheeks in, prune-like.

Hopelessly, I made a last-ditch effort: "But if we really worked on her — makeup, clothes —"

"Jen, whatever you make her look like, Maude Harris still has about as much personality as a bar of laundry soap," Larry said.

"You're just a bunch of macho skunks!" I whacked at them, trying to keep from crying because the idea of changing Maude's life suddenly meant so much to me, but it seemed impossible to convince them; tears burned my eyes. Ashamed, I ran from the campfire toward the old iron bridge.

Larry came after me and put his hand on my shoulder, but I shook him off, staring down at the river where stars trembled in the dark current. "You're serious," he said, "about Maude Harris?"

I nodded. He touched my hair. "Okay," he said, "I'll go along with it."

"I don't want you to just go along with it!"

It was so frustrating, because I couldn't make them see what the experiment could mean to someone as lonely as Maude. Then suddenly I realized how to convince them, and I excitedly pulled Larry back to the campfire.

"Imagine," I said, "Maude Harris becomes *in* with the most *in* clique at Lakeside High, namely us. It'll shock the socks off all the phonies in the school and they'll come buzzing around Maude, figuring she's got to have some ultra-hidden attractions. Once they start looking at her differently, and she starts looking at herself differently, it's like we'll be hypnotizing the whole school!"

Slowly the idea dawned on them, and the boys started grinning, nodding, and chuckling.

"Oh, man, I get it! First everybody thinks we've gone bananas chasing Maude, but then they end up imitating us because they all want to be *in*."

"Hey, just like *The Emperor's New Clothes!*"

"Dynamite idea for a Broadway musical!"

"We'll be showing up the whole school system!" Larry said dramatically. "We'll be doing what the system should have done for somebody like Maude a long time ago."

When Larry said that, I felt all my conflicts about him disappear totally — almost. My only fear was that the boys might not take the experiment seriously, and so I made a condition that none of us should do anything to hurt Maude in any way, and we shouldn't just think of her as some guinea pig to make ourselves big shots. The guys nodded gravely and said they agreed, including a promise to stay with the experiment until at least graduation and never to reveal it to anyone, even Maude herself, but I didn't know how to be sure they all meant it.

We put out the campfire and I snuggled next to Larry all the way home in the truck. The four of us said good-bye at my house, hugging a big four-person hug. We had a terrific feeling, as if we all had a mission to accomplish, and I completely forgot my concern that we might hurt Maude in some way.

So at midnight I found myself alone in the house, with a nice note from my folks about their going off to some fund-raising party. I went to bed sort of depressed again, because you expect you might at least see your mother and father when you come back after two months away, but then I thought of Maude Harris and the experiment, our experiment, and my blues vanished.

At least for a while.

Two

Maude

The first time Jen Robbins ever stood face to face with me, I spilled half a cup of luke-warm apple cider on her gray suede shoes.

It seems silly that another girl my own age could affect me the way Jen did, but I was horribly shy. And Jen was — Jen. When she appeared without any warning at the door of my house, I couldn't believe my eyes. How did I spill the cider on her? Would you believe it was caused by Doctor Strange, Master of the Mystic Arts?

It happened when I was trying a new apple nut loaf recipe from my new cookbook and also helping Mark and Stevie do their homework. Helping my brothers meant mostly urging them, urging meant nagging. In the kitchen I oiled two loaf pans, ready to start softening the yeast in the cider. Then I heard an evil-sounding laugh and I tiptoed to the boys' room, cider in hand.

Facing me was a lurid comic book cover: *Doctor Strange, The Master Magician's Most Bizarre Battles!* Behind the cover, nine-year-old Mark was reading to Stevie, a year younger, Mark cackling wickedly.

Can arithmetic ever compete against stories like "Domain of the Dread Dormammu" and "Return of the Omnipotent Baron Mordo"? I hated to, but I took the comic book away.

"Oh, Maude, please please, just one more page!"

"After your homework."

Mark, skinny and blonde, made a ferocious disgusted face at me. Chunky little Stevie scratched his head with a sad, terribly disappointed face. They knew how to make me feel guilty. Mark groaned, "You always spoil our fun!"

Walking away with the comic book, I was on the verge of giving it back, but the doorbell rang. That's why I was standing there with half a cup of lukewarm cider in one hand and a copy of *Doctor Strange* in the other, when I opened the door and Jen Robbins, queen of last year's junior class, made my knees turn to water.

"Hi!" she said cheerfully, "I've got some fascinating things to show you."

I knew I was supposed to say something, but nothing came out of my mouth. Jen was wearing a pearl gray suit, gray suede high-heeled shoes, a silky blouse open at the throat, beautiful but businesslike. In school I'd watched her from a distance, breezing around the halls like a movie star with her own special magic, though she never acted high and mighty. She was my age but she acted so fearless and mature I felt much younger. You'd see her in the lunchroom wearing huge gold earrings, a gypsy blouse, a daring slit skirt, and then the next day tight black pants, a black pullover, high shiny clogs, a dozen bright rings. I had never dared to meet her eyes or talk to her.

"Say, don't I know you from Lakeside High?" Jen lightheartedly filled in my awkward silence.

Open your mouth, say something, Maude! I sent a definite message to my brain. The message did not reach my mouth.

"Aren't you a senior this year?" Jen went on brightly. "I'm Jen Robbins."

She extended her hand to me. I'd seen girls shake hands that way and envied them. I wanted to reach out to put my hand into her grip. She had such a friendly smile and her hand was hanging in midair. Suddenly my hand shot out from my side, and with it the half cup of lukewarm apple cider. A shower of cider made dark blotches on Jen's skirt and gray suede shoes.

"Oh, no!" I cried. Stupidly, I brushed at her skirt and shoes with the *Doctor Strange* book, flapping it jerkily.

"Hey, don't worry!" she said, but her smile was a little strained this time.

"Now I remember," she added, relaxing. "Your name is Maude Harris, isn't it?"

I managed to produce something vaguely resembling a nod, but I was sure she could see my face muscles twitching away.

"I'm selling beauty products door to door," Jen explained, "also jewelry."

Of course, her attractive leather case obviously carried sample products. I was a little disappointed, but mostly relieved, to find out that Jen had come to my house by chance and not just to see me.

"I have some free samples for you and your mother."

My mind was trying to tell Jen that my mother Nancy was no longer alive, but the words got stuck. For some unknown reason I suddenly wanted to blurt out: *Nancy wasn't my real mother. The court wouldn't let my real mother keep me. Nancy and Dad adopted me. Nancy loved me. Nancy died.*

What an idiot I felt like, standing there in front of Jen, who obviously expected me to ask her inside, and me a lump blocking the doorway, yet Jen seemed so at ease, as if she really liked me in spite of my paralyzing embarrassment. Of course, a good salesperson would have to be that way, I thought, uncharitably.

"I guess this isn't a good time for you, Maude. What about tomorrow? I've got some super bargains, Maude."

Finally, I managed to say, "Oh, I'm so sorry."

"Why?" Her face was pretty with surprise.

"Your shoes," I mumbled. "My apple cider."

Jen threw her head back and laughed, so free and easy, just watching her made me feel good. But I knew I'd never be able to laugh that way, so confident.

"I was going to throw these shoes away anyway." Jen winked at me. "Well, so long, Maude. Maybe I'll see you in school tomorrow."

I closed the door, caught between glad and sad. Glad to stop making a fool of myself, sad I'd lost a chance to start a . . . start a what? Friendship? Me? With Jen Robbins?

I breathed a sigh of relief and marched back to my apple nut loaf recipe.

What had Jen said? Maybe she'd see me in school tomorrow? Would she and I actually talk again? Eat lunch together? Take a walk together; share our thoughts; become friends. Maybe through Jen I'd meet lots of boys.

"No!" I banged my fist on the table. "You are who you are, and stay that way!"

I knew I'd always be the Maude Harris who dropped lukewarm apple cider on Jen Robbins's shoes. Maybe she'd say hello to me because she felt sorry, but I didn't want that. What did I have to offer someone like Jen? Anyway, when someone says out of pure politeness that maybe she'll see you in school, it means nothing.

Wednesday I saw Jen again, this time near the principal's office. I darted away up the nearest staircase, terrified she might say hello to me in the middle of a bunch of her friends, and I would stand there, a gibbering idiot.

Friday, in the supermarket, we almost met again. Larry Meadows, Dolph Krager, and

Wayne Grants were with her. They were near the frozen pizzas, and I was reaching for a box of Cap'n Crunch breakfast cereal the boys had begged for. I could have sworn Jen saw me. I dropped the Cap'n Crunch, flew down the aisle, knocked over a pyramid of toilet paper, and ran into the street until my breath gave out. Ridiculous? Sure, but I was scared to get anywhere near Jen.

Still, I kept chewing over every word that had passed between us. "Maybe I'll see you, Maude . . ."

I had long ago given up on ever having the things other girls seemed to get so easily: meeting boys, talking with a circle of girls, going for long car rides, laughing together in the movies, sharing the thrill of a rock concert with friends. Speaking to Jen in my doorway had opened up all these desires like an old wound. I almost hated her for it but I couldn't.

Then, on Saturday, I was near the kitchen window, a load of sewing before me, but smiling because I liked to watch Stevie dodge away from Mark's clutches in the backyard between the small young plum tree and the huge old pine. A smell of simmering vegetable soup and roasting chicken filled the kitchen. My mother Nancy had taught me to cook after she adopted me. I was six, a few years before the boys were born, when Nancy brought me home to my own room overlooking the golf course. Before Nancy, I remembered only a blur of unpleasant foster homes.

Thoughts of Jen Robbins flickered around

the edges of my mind. Try to think of something else, I told myself. Your life is okay the way it is, Maude. The boys would eat supper; I'd put them to sleep; Dad would come home late from doing inventory at the store and I'd heat up his food and enjoy the sight of him digging into his favorite dishes.

I lingered at the kitchen window. Would Jen Robbins spend her time cooking, sewing, watching out for two younger brothers? Actually, Mark and Stevie could already make their own breakfasts. Except when Mark had a nosebleed or Stevie was scared of the dark, they were very independent: could do the laundry, go shopping, defrost the refrigerator. Soon they would hardly need me. What was I supposed to do with my life? In nine months I'd graduate from Lakeside. Then what? College? I couldn't face living with a lot of kids in a dorm. Would Dad ever remarry? Not likely. I could be his housekeeper the rest of my life, or get a job in a quiet corner of some office. I didn't want much for myself. Jen Robbins probably wanted the whole world.

These were some of my thoughts when a girl's voice — I didn't recognize it was Jen Robbins — screamed in pain from the front of our house.

"Help! Help!"

Someone sounded agonized. I dropped my sewing and dashed toward the front door. Emergencies were my best times; I didn't have to think or worry about doing or saying the right thing. I raced out the door and there was Jen Robbins, sprawled on the sidewalk, her face tight with pain, groaning. One foot twisted under the chain of her ten-speed bicycle.

Her voice came out cracked and hurting: "My ankle! My ankle!"

Maybe I should have been suspicious, but I was too excited and flustered. My nervousness tripled, seeing Larry Meadows, Dolph Krager, and Wayne Grants come speeding around the corner on bicycles, shouting: "Hey, Jen! Wait up, you maniac! Stop, thief!" as if Jen had zoomed ahead of them for fun.

An instant later they jumped off their bikes in alarm. She was moaning on the ground. They reached her the same time I did, and nodded gratefully at me as if I'd been helping her. Gently, they got her untwisted from the bike, and the next thing I knew I was leading them through the front door and into my living room. I brought ice immediately and we packed her ankle, which didn't look swollen but seemed to be killing her. Then my panic set in.

The most popular seniors in Lakeside High, in my house! I couldn't face trying to talk to all four of them. My mouth opened and words shot out. "Ace bandage . . . her ankle . . . my father always . . . when somebody . . . I'll get one . . . I'll . . . the drugstore!"

I ran right out of the house, heading down the street for the drugstore, praying that when I returned they somehow would all have disappeared.

Three

Jen

When I knocked on Maude's door, pretending to sell her my line of beauty aids, and she stood there with her jaw unhinged, a good feeling shot through me that I was really needed by this poor girl. If hair could speak, her hair would have been shrieking "Help!" because the dark braids were pulled so painfully tight in circles on her head. I had this *urge* to yank her hair free of the braids and let it hang loose, especially since the hair would do such a nice job of covering her ears, which definitely were too large. Trying to revolutionize Maude's life, I was getting obsessed with every detail, like a general figuring strategy for a campaign.

I hunted through my collection of beauty magazines and found some sensational faces of those French and Italian actresses who have really *significant* noses and give you the impression of gorgeous lady spies. That's how I got the idea that the right image for Maude might be ultra-ultra-mysterious, and instead of those baggy, shapeless dresses maybe some really dramatic slinky clothes in rich dark colors.

Obviously I was a real believer in beauty culture. People had no idea how many hours I spent doing myself just the way I guess an artist does a painting. Even when I wore an old T-shirt, patched dungarees, and dirty sneakers, believe me I checked every detail.

Anyway, after I got my first long, close view of Maude, the next step was that charade with my fake twisted ankle on her front lawn. I never expected Maude to race out of her own house with her tail between her legs on the pretext of getting an Ace bandage, leaving us alone with her collie, who didn't seem to mind. We stood there shrugging our shoulders, Larry, Dolph, Wayne, and I.

"Looks to me like Maude was on her way to Afghanistan." Larry shook his head doubtfully.

"And we'll probably get arrested for housebreaking." Wayne fluttered his eyelashes in my direction.

"I ain't so all-fired happy about parkin' my carcass in some stranger's livin' room," Dolph muttered.

"Maude isn't really a stranger," I argued.

"She may not be a stranger" — Wayne wrinkled his nose — "but she sure is strange."

"I say we saddle up and vamoose!" Dolph croaked. "That there Maude filly is a little loco between the ears."

"You can't!" I burst out. "You promised!"

"Well, I didn't know what I was getting

into." Dolph moodily dropped his Western accent, which usually meant he wouldn't change his mind if Mt. Vesuvius fell on him. "I've seen merry-go-round horses with more to say than Maude Harris!"

"That's what makes it a challenge, Dolph," Larry said soothingly, persuasively, and I was grateful to him for trying.

"Yeah, you've got nothing to lose, you and Jen. But *me* — I've got enough woman trouble without chasing Maude Harris!"

Shrewdly, Larry said, "When a guy is a football star like you and he dates a girl like Maude, the whole student body will start thinking that this guy must be really *deep*, you know, because he's looking below the surface at the real character in the girl."

Mournfully, Dolph said, "All I want is Mary Jane Jackson, and she's going steady with that turnip who talks like he's Albert Einstein."

Dolph turned a long stubborn look in my direction. I suppose he saw something in my face that affected him — my disappointment — and his mouth softened. "Well, hoss" — he furrowed his brow at me — "seein' as how you aims to lasso that Maude critter, reckon I'll still be part of the posse."

At that moment two little boys wearing football uniforms whammed through the front door and stopped dead, staring at the four of us like we were purple people-eaters from planet X.

"You guys must be Maude's brothers,"

Larry said. "Hey, Dolph, think Coach Berg-man will let these two jocks sit on the bench when we play Jefferson High next month?"

The two boys went goggle-eyed when they learned that Larry was quarterback and Dolph the star runner for Lakeside High. In no time, Maude's brothers were tackling Larry and Dolph and Wayne in the back-yard, screeching "Pass it!" and "Block him!" and "Run!" just as if they had known each other all their lives, which sometimes makes me jealous — the way boys get together in a game and suddenly they are lifelong buddies.

Myself, I stayed in the house to try to dig up whatever I could about Maude that could help us in the experiment. If I felt sneaky peeking around her house, I convinced my-self it was all for her own good. Maude's room was a shock. I couldn't believe any sev-enteen-year-old girl alive owned so few dresses and shoes and absolutely no makeup, no sexy underwear or bikinis, no hi-fi or record albums or 8-track stereo, no posters. My heart sank, maybe Maude *was* a hopeless case. Then Maude's collie rubbed up under my hand, wanting me to pet her, and I combed my fingers gently through her flow-ing white mane. There had to be hope for Maude. On Maude's desk there was a little plastic rabbit with a pink nose, and a green glass Buddha. On the wall was a photograph of a handsome woman with the inscription: "For Maude, with love, Mother." Quickly, I rifled through the papers on Maude's desk and in her drawers and found her school program and copied it so I would know where she was every period of every day in Lakeside High.

Dolph and Wayne and Larry had Maude's brothers eating out of their hands by the time I managed to get myself stretched out on the sofa with my fake twisted ankle, moments before Maude walked, or you might say stumbled, into the house and dropped the Ace bandage into Dolph's big paw. Before I could get my tongue in motion, she skittered away to the kitchen and we were all left with these enormous, magnetic, loving smiles glued on our faces that we hoped were beginning to work some kind of psychological magic on Maude.

Larry silently hooked his thumb toward the street, but I was determined to force Maude to make real physical contact with all the guys. I trooped them into the kitchen, hopping behind them with my phony sore ankle and told her we just wanted to say good-bye. This is Wayne, this is Dolph, this is Larry, each of them shaking her hand. I felt like a total sadist, causing the tortured timid look in her eyes.

Afterward, at home alone in my bedroom gluing on a new set of false fingernails, I remembered the fright in Maude's eyes and decided we'd better not pressure her too much or we'd scare her into a nervous breakdown. Three quick phone calls and I told each of the guys we should go easy, not rush things with Maude. I set up a sort of schedule, using her school program so that one or another of us would make contact with her accidentally-on-purpose several times each day, just a smile or a wave or a hello, and maybe she'd let her guard down little by little. I was pretty proud of myself the way I arranged Dolph or Wayne running into her in the library or outside her homeroom, or Larry and I passing her near her math class. My biggest ploy was pulling strings to have my program changed so I could be in Maude's music class, where I nodded and smiled but kept my distance. Day by day she seemed a thousandth of an inch less uptight.

One nice thing was that my insomnia stopped. Probably not real insomnia, but since my junior year I'd wake up two or three times a night, my nerves racing to go somewhere and do something, anything but lie there, and I'd shuffle around the house, muttering loudly, half wishing my parents would open their bedroom door and yell at me. But my mother slept with those fat pink wax globs stuffed in her ears, and my father was so exhausted from business trips and dinner parties you could drive a fire truck across his forehead and he'd probably mumble, "Just another five minutes, huh, honey?"

My only uncertainty was whether or not it bugged Larry that I was sort of running the experiment with Maude. He didn't actually complain but we did have an argument that upset me more than I admitted. I was writing a note to Larry in Mr. Palkowsky's class, Problems of World Hygiene. Rivers poisoned, forests cut down, the ozone layer disappearing.

My note to Larry said: "We should wait a few weeks before we ask M. to see a movie or such. Then a few weeks more before D. or W. asks her for a date. You look very h-n-s-me this morning."

Larry scribbled an answer, balled it up, popped it across to me. I uncrumpled his note: "Disagree. M. needs earthquake. D. and W. *both* should ask for dates *this week.* P.S. I like yesterday's perfume better. Your friend, Mr. Perfect."

I was always hoping that Larry would tell me I was be-ut-ful: he never did. But what truly upset me was the danger that Larry and Dolph and Wayne would move too fast with Maude. Two sentences into another note to Larry, my ballpoint pen died of thirst, and the bell sounded ending the class.

In the hallway, Larry and I walked together real close, him wearing that spicy toilet water I had given him for his eighteenth birthday. My feelings did a roller coaster from medium rotten to wanting him so much to kiss me and kiss me. In moments like this, I thought our relationship was pure magic and would be a forever of doing things together, sharing exciting ideas, and looking into each other's eyes.

"We should have a name for this whole thing with Maude." Larry grinned and jumped airily down an entire flight of stairs as if it were nothing. My emotions absolutely shriveled. I hated that macho stuff, although

29

on the football field the cheerleader in me ate it up.

"We'll call it The Great Lakeside High Experiment!" Larry snickered.

"You shouldn't snicker about it. Her life is at stake."

"I didn't snicker," Larry grunted. "What a creepo word!"

"It sounded to me like a definite snicker."

"Anyway, who gave you the right to judge my snickers?"

Whereas a moment before I was aching for him to kiss me, now ice cubes formed. "You wouldn't snicker if you took this experiment seriously."

"Dig yourself, Jen! You sound like some robot social worker."

I would have bet anything he was reacting because he didn't like a girl practically directing the whole experiment, but I knew I'd better keep my mouth shut. Larry could be so sensitive one moment and so dense the next.

Standing at the turn of the staircase, not a person in sight, I was already late for my gym class, but Larry's eyes glittered and his arm snaked around my waist, pulling me close to him, and even though I didn't want to, I let him kiss me. Why is it you feel like a jerk or a prude or just plain mean, selfish, and miserly when a boy you care about wants some affection from you and the way he goes about it somehow turns you off — like the hint of coldness in his eyes or a roughness and haste in the way he grabs you?

I had a vague premonition, as if my future
with Larry depended on what happened to
Maude, because Larry and I were really
working together for the first time and if we
couldn't share it successfully, then we
weren't a real team. I didn't like to think
about ever being without Larry, owing to the
fact that it made my nervous system go hay-
wire.

Four

Maude

I couldn't seem to avoid them. In school several times a day one or another of them would notice me and nod or smile or wave or say "Hi!" or "Hi, Maude!" One time Wayne winked at me as he passed me near the ceramics shop and I got so flustered I walked nose first into a swinging door.

They were trying to be nice to me. How could they know it made me feel so bad? I'd never had a boyfriend or a girl friend. I'd learned to be alone. It hurt when they smiled at me. I prayed they would forget I existed.

One night I stood talking to myself in front of the bathroom mirror. "You look a little sick. If you get sick you won't have to go to school. You won't have to see *them*. If your face was different maybe you wouldn't mind seeing them. Maybe you're coming down with the flu." I stuck out my tongue at myself in the mirror. It was a decent tongue, small, pink, smooth.

A small voice interrupted me. "Why are

32

you talking to yourself in the mirror?" It was Stevie, staring at me.

"Because I'm ugly."

"If you're ugly, why look at yourself?"

"Maybe I'm not *that* ugly."

"Well, you're fairly ugly."

"Thanks."

"I think *most* girls are fairly ugly."

That night, in bed, I decided I would force myself to act more normal when Jen or Larry or Wayne or Dolph greeted me. Just wave back or say "Hi!" and leave it at that.

My first opportunity came on the down staircase near the typing room. Larry and Wayne came snaking illegally upward through the flow of boys and girls. They each threw a quick salute at me as they came past. Lamebrain that I am, I waved back with the hand supporting my books. My books went bouncing down the steps, pages from a loose-leaf exploding in every direction.

It was hopeless. *I* was hopeless. One disaster after another. Yet I couldn't forget the experience I'd had that day in my kitchen when Jen had introduced me.

"This is Dolph Krager, Maude," Jen had said, and Dolph had reached down and surrounded my limp hand in his huge warm paw. I tried to pull my hand away, but he wouldn't let go. He was so tall, soft brown hair and eyes.

"Howdy, Maude," he said confidently.

Dolph held onto my hand and passed it

over to Wayne. Wayne's touch was moist, electric, gave me goose pimples. His dark liquid eyes, large black pupils — so intense.

Wayne handed my hand over to Larry. Larry gave my hand a friendly squeeze. With him I felt more relaxed, perhaps because everybody in school knew he and Jen were practically engaged, so he was safe. I liked his sandy hair, which fell over his forehead, and the lightest sprinkling of honey-colored freckles on his nose and cheekbones.

"We promised your brothers," Larry said, his eyes so directly at me I got shaky again, "that they could sit on the sidelines when we play the first Lakeside game."

I couldn't relate to that. Me bringing Mark and Stevie to my first football game ever? Larry the quarterback, Dolph the star runner, Jen cheerleading, people staring at Mark and Stevie and me?

Going to bed that night, Mark and Stevie argued about who would sleep with the football.

"People don't sleep with footballs," I said.

"Larry's father wanted *him* to sleep with a football," Stevie spouted.

"Will you take us to meet Larry's coach and maybe sit on the bench with the football players?" Mark begged.

"Oh, please please please please, Maude, huh?" Stevie added.

I said yes, I would take them to the game. Then we tossed a coin to see who would sleep with the football. Mark won.

Once the boys were asleep, I went outside through the back door for some fresh air. Linda rubbed against me. She wanted to go running. I stood there between the dark presence of the plum tree and the high black branches of the pine. The trees smelled of rain. I wrapped my arms around myself, staring up at the stars. Lonely stars traveling at fantastic speeds, yet peaceful, motionless. I had thought my world was neat and tidy and quiet, standing still with empty, safe, dark space all around. Then Larry and Jen and the others came like meteors whipping past me, tugging me out of my orbit. The leaves whispered on the plum tree. I shivered, tightened my arms around myself. I realized that I was hugging myself. I wondered how a boy's arms felt.

Then I went upstairs to my room and dug around in the mess at the bottom of my closet until I found last year's school newspapers, which I had saved for no reason. The *Lakeside High School Times*. I flipped through the pages and bent down the corners of the ones I wanted. With a scissor I sliced through the dry old papers, cutting out three photographs and then a fourth. A picture of Jen leading a cheer — white boots, tiny skirt, fluffy pompoms — at last year's state championship game. Lakeside had lost. A photo of Wayne at last year's student dance, arms around his guitar, mouth wide open inches from the microphone. A picture of Dolph smashing toward me with the football. Larry, also in his football uniform, caught by the camera as the ball went whipping out of his hand.

I held the four photographs in the palm of my hand. Then I spread them out on the rug beside my bed and stared. All four of them looked so magical to me, yet so natural. I felt a twisting hunger inside me that hurt.

Snatching up the photographs, I crumpled them all together, ran downstairs to the fire-place, threw them in, and lighted a match to them. Flames ate up the faces. Suddenly I tried to grab the burning pictures out of the fireplace, but too late. The faces were nothing but charred black ash. I went to the kitchen and washed my fingers in the dark.

"That you, Maude?"

The front door closed. My father. "Maude?" The kitchen light flashed on. Dad had been to a Reserve Officers' meeting and the gold captain's bars on his uniform seemed out of place among my pots and pans.

"Did I hear you crying?"

"No," I said, heating up the spaghetti for him.

He washed his hands. Sat down. There were dark circles under his eyes. That look on his face meant he was thinking about Nancy.

"Good spaghetti. Good sauce."

"Thanks, Dad."

"But I think Nancy used more garlic."

"Oh."

"Don't forget to use more garlic next time."

"I won't."

"Making any friends, Maude? No, don't tell me. Not going to push you. Move at your own pace."

He leaned across the table toward me. "Do you miss her?" He sank back into himself. " 'Course you do. Sometimes I can't believe Nancy's gone."

I finished the dishes. Dad got into bed and fell asleep over some business letters. I turned out his light.

Ten minutes later Linda and I squeezed through our hole in the fence to the golf course behind our house, deserted under the new moon. Linda pranced over the smooth curves of grass between the golf tees. Just the two of us in all that emptiness, racing together on the short thick grass and through the sand traps. Something in me responded to speed. I could let go. We were free. Maude Harris didn't exist anymore. Only the running. It wasn't a girl and a dog running. It had a magic. I flew ahead of Linda, darting from side to side, escaping her, letting her almost catch me. Barefoot in the summer, sneakers in the fall or spring, heavy boots in winter — we never failed to run together at night. Effortless. No one knew. Afterward we'd sit a while in the emptiness.

Later, sliding into bed, with Linda on the coverlet, my fingers throbbed a little from the burn I'd gotten when I grabbed the newspaper pictures out of the fire. Jen, Larry, Dolph, Wayne.

Well, what began happening in school and at home was that I started having a lot more accidents than usual. I mean, I was normally a very accident-prone person anyway, but I got much worse when Jen and the boys started paying attention to me. At home, black smoke belched from chickens broiled beyond recognition and sweet potatoes baked into lumps of bituminous coal. The bathtub overflowed, wet laundry was forgotten in the washer and mildewed, and there was more than the usual number of dropped and broken glasses and mugs. In school, in chemistry lab, I knocked over a Bunsen burner and scorched Mr. Bingham's pants. In gym I accidentally swung one of the flying rings and hit the substitute teacher in the back of her head. She claimed I did it on purpose.

"You've been having quite a few accidents, Maude. Like to tell me about them?" Mrs. Fisher had me in her office. A plump little lady with nice laugh lines around her eyes. The document on her wall said Edna Fisher, Certified School Psychologist.

"Maude, I can't help you unless you want to be helped."

She also had spaces between her teeth. I wanted to trust her laugh lines and the spaces between her teeth, but I couldn't. My actual opinion about why I was accident-prone was that I was born with a basically sloppy nervous system. I could have told Mrs. Fisher that when I was seven and only recently adopted by Nancy, I slipped and crashed down on the roof of a three-hundred-dollar antique doll house belonging to a girl I desperately wanted to be my friend. Well, Mrs. Fisher did a bunch of talking and I did a bigger bunch of saying nothing.

Think positive was the gist of Mrs. Fisher's advice. Shuffling out of her office, I first tried to think positive about thinking positive. All that good advice had made me very thirsty, so I bent down at the water fountain near the fire extinguisher. With the water splashing into my mouth, I caught a glimpse of the two Bianchi sisters way down the hall, chattering away with Wayne and Dolph. The Bianchi sisters were twins, sexy girls with round fruity bodies that caused boys to write a large number of very unpleasant graffiti on the school walls. Also in the hall, near the middle staircase, were some friends of Jen: Carol Duarte, Gail Roddy, and Mindy Schwartz. What happened next made me wish I could shrink to the size of an aspirin.

"Hey, Maude!" Dolph yelled, and Wayne with him.

The two of them left the Bianchi sisters flat and started in my direction. Water splashing against my teeth, I watched in horrified fascination as the two boys practically sprinted down the hall toward me. The girls gaped in disbelief. The water from the fountain went straight up my nose and also soaked the sleeve of my dress.

"Ah been out brandin' calves since sunup, Maude," Dolph said loudly, "and ah shore do need some frontier woman friendliness."

Wayne shoved good-naturedly past Dolph, who was at least a hundred pounds bigger.

"Maude, you will flip out when you read my new lyrics for 'Rise from the Dead.'"

The two of them surrounded me, talking back and forth to me and each other. Wayne held a sheet of lyrics for me to read and also hummed the melody. Dolph kept asking me questions and answering them for me. I attempted a smile, but my upper and lower teeth felt glued together. I was sure my face looked lopsided. Yet even though I was speechless, it seemed as if the three of us were having a real, ordinary, interesting, mutual conversation. But when I saw all the girls staring at us, I prayed that a black hole would open in the floor and swallow me.

At the same time there was a giddy sensation of being desired. Dolph and Wayne swept me along between them. I could not believe it was me they were looking at the way boys look at girls in movies. They could have waltzed me out the third floor window and I would have followed them gladly.

Then two black words hit me right between the eyes: GIRLS' BATHROOM. I darted away from Dolph and Wayne and flung myself into the bathroom. No one was there. Breathless with excitement, my heart pounding and pounding, I locked myself inside a cubicle and stood there frozen. Then my face suddenly burst open into a smile so big it hurt my skin. It was a smile that must have been hiding for years. A stupid, foolish, happy smile that seemed to start somewhere in my solar plexus and stretch all the way from my eyes to my ears and around my head. Also, my eyes were producing lots of tears. Glad tears.

I waited inside the bathroom until I heard the signal for the beginning of the next class. I pushed open the door. No one was in sight.

Daydreaming my way down to the second floor, I slipped into my trigonometry class. Math was my best subject. Math gave me a sense of safety. Straight lines, triangles, equations — they took me away from the Maude Harris I didn't like. A square root was a square root. The nice thing was, I made very few mistakes in math, apart from occasionally stabbing myself with a compass point or tripping and crushing a balsa wood trapezohedron under my elbow.

Trig over, I almost didn't go to music because I knew Jen was in the class. Sure enough, she slipped a note onto my desk. Why didn't I just calmly open it and read what she wrote? It wasn't going to bite me, but maybe it was. All period I sat there with her note in front of me. At the bell I was the first one out the door.

Churned up about Jen and her note, happy and a little dazed about my experience with Wayne and Dolph, but more scared than ever, I scurried out a side entrance of the school. Please don't let me meet any of *them*, I thought. Knots of kids jammed the sidewalk. Boys in rebuilt cars raced their engines, honked their horns. Car radios and portable cassette players slaughtered your ears. Halfway down the block, I saw Jen. I turned around and headed the other way, hoping she hadn't noticed me.

I was ashamed but I couldn't help it. I walked faster, praying she'd stop with one of the groups of seniors. Glancing back through the crowd, I saw her still behind me. She waved. I tripped, dropped my books, scrambled to grab them. I hurried as quickly as possible without actually running. A red light stopped me. Sweat broke out all over my body. Jen shouted my name. I threw myself into the traffic, cars whipping past me on both sides. and dodged across onto the sidewalk. Jen followed! My legs started pumping up and down. I couldn't believe she was chasing me! And then it rained. And then I escaped. I lost her. Only then I realized how much I had wanted her to catch me.

Five

Jen

Eating in the school cafeteria you needed ears of stone and a stainless steel stomach to survive. I was hedged in by Carol Duarte, chairman of the senior prom committee; and Gail Roddy, a cheerleader; and Mindy Schwartz, assistant editor of the school paper.

"As I was saying," Mindy announced, pencil in her hair, à la Jane Fonda girl journalist, her idol, "Dolph and Wayne saw Maude Harris and they dropped those two Bianchi sisters cold and moved in on Maude with the gloppiest smiles you ever saw."

Then Carol, who had never gotten over her feelings for Wayne, threw her two cents in, with a few sparks of anger. "Why would Dolph or Wayne or *anyone* want to talk to Maude Harris? She's got about as much glamour as a stop sign!"

"Maybe her father is an internationally dangerous dope-seller." Gail put on her fake dumb-cheerleader look, "and he's in hiding from Interpol, so Maude is really his wildly

43

sexy daughter who has disguised herself as a klutz to protect her father from capture."

We all booed loudly. Gail took a bow.

"Jen" — Mindy eyed me shrewdly — "you know Dolph and Wayne better than any of us. What's *with* them?"

"I can't figure it out," I said innocently, getting a kick from seeing them each so mystified.

By the time I walked from the cafeteria to Miss Passwassel's English honors class, I was patting myself mentally on the back. Mindy, Gail, and Carol would soon have the entire school buzzing.

In music I passed a note to Maude and she sat there with my note unopened for the entire period. It said: "I've got a problem you could really help me with. Can we talk after school? Jen."

Actually, I had no idea what problem I meant; I'd think of something for sure. Only, Maude sitting there minute after minute, her eyes focused on Mr. Welch and paying no attention whatsoever to my note got me fuming, so when the period ended and Maude zipped out I stood there in the emptying classroom and my blood was boiling. My note was still sitting on her desk. She hadn't even been polite enough to read it! She'd let her empty little life go down the drain in spite of the very people who wanted to help her! I got so worked up that I took off after her, determined to catch her, ask her why she didn't read my note, get an answer out of her!

Out on the sidewalk, I caught sight of Maude's head bobbing through the crowd half a block away. Eyes on Maude, I weaved through the swarming kids. Some threw me big hellos, but my concentration was totally on Maude, hurrying past the motorcycles and souped-up cars, until somebody grabbed my wrist. "Jen!" It was Larry.

Thoughtlessly, I tore my wrist free and snapped at him, "Not now!" He looked ready to slap me, but I didn't wait to explain because I saw Maude, at the far corner, dive into traffic against the light, a bus just missing her.

She glanced back over her shoulder in my direction. I waved at her. She quickened her pace away from me. And the faster I walked after her, the faster she pumped her shoes on the concrete. Ultra-stubborn jerk that I was, instead of just stopping and letting her go take a flying leap, I shouted her name down the street: "Maude! Wait!" She jumped like a frightened rabbit and began to run, not walk. I yanked off my high-heeled shoes and raced after her with this compulsion to grab her by the shoulders and shake some sense into her, even if it ruined the whole experiment. Suddenly rain came down, drops the size of your eyeball, and I was getting soaked but couldn't stop, barefoot in hot pursuit past a chain drugstore, and I was tempted to shout, "Stop, thief!" as if Maude was a mugger.

She ducked into an alley that led out through the parking lot of a shopping center, and I couldn't believe how fast she was running, or how ridiculous it was. I was losing ground rapidly, but running made her a completely different, graceful person, her rain-soaked dress, usually so baggy, clinging to her body so you could tell her figure had possibilities. Then there was a grassy field and a gang of trees parallel to the highway and Maude put on an impossible burst of speed and disappeared through the rain and the trees.

I stopped dead, a five-alarm fire in my lungs, suddenly sick to my stomach, and feeling like the world's perfect fool.

A finger poked my shoulder, hard. I turned, saw Larry's eyes fixed on me, both of us dripping wet. "You followed me!" I croaked accusingly, gulping for air.

Firmly, he lifted me up, sat me on the hood of a parked car, and wiped my face with his handkerchief.

He insisted on paying for a cab. We didn't say much. Inside the house, as usual, no sign of my parents. Our guest room was practically his second home, so he had a change of clothes there. While I poured us each a cup of coffee, I said, "Ask me why I need a good geologist!"

"Okay, why?"

"Because I must have rocks in my head, chasing Maude barefoot."

"I've never seen you take anything so seriously." He had a charming little-boy look on his face.

"Let me give you a butterfly kiss," I said. "Close your eyes."

He closed his eyes warily and I blinked my eyelashes against his lips, tickling until he cracked up and closed his arms tight around me. His mouth on my mouth, he kissed me in a way that he knew I didn't like because it felt too dangerous.

I asked, "Will you help me with Maude?"

"Haven't I been?" Larry held my face in his hands. "Why is it so important for you to help Maude?"

I didn't have an answer for him.

"Just don't forget you're in love with me," he murmured.

We kissed and kissed, long, slow kisses.

"What's going to happen to us, Larry, after graduation?" I whispered against his ear.

"College. I don't know. Maybe a football scholarship. You could come with me."

"Do you want me to?"

"Do you *want* to?"

I heard a key in the front door. Probably Mom. She'd be delighted that Larry was here.

It might be easier, I thought rebelliously, to be like Maude Harris, a female hermit or something.

Six

Maude

Dear Jen, Running away from you in the rain was one of the most ?????????? experiences of my life. It left me feeling so ??????????

I tore the note to scraps. She deserved a *real* apology.

On Monday morning I waited in the park opposite Jen's house. Coming alone out of her front door, she didn't notice me. Her pants were of some shiny metallic material so tight they showed every curve of her legs; a tight jacket was of the same stuff, and a white beret made her look very French.

Twice I cleared my throat to call her but my voice failed. On my third try I produced a sound: "Jen!"

Not a sign that she was surprised to see me. She waited for me to catch up. She wasn't quite smiling, but the way she arranged her mouth told me she was glad to see me.

48

"Hi, Jen."

"Hi, Maude."

Was I grateful she didn't ask me what I was doing there!

She walked with long free strides. I fell in step beside her. She didn't say a word. I was depending on her to do all the talking. She always had so much to say — jokes and interesting gossip or new ideas. Why was she silent? Angry at me? Or maybe she knew I had something to say and wanted to give me a chance to say it.

"Jen?" I said.

"That's me," she said, yet I knew she wasn't being sarcastic because her voice was patient.

"I want to say something."

"Go ahead."

"It's important."

"Sure."

"Well . . ."

The sun was jumping in the trees as we walked.

"I'm sorry, Jen." I finally squeezed the words out.

"Huh?" Her eyebrows were bent in a puzzled expression.

"The other day, after school, running away when you called me, I'm sorry." I watched Jen's face for some response.

"Oh, that's okay, Maude."

What was she thinking? She wasn't taking it very seriously, so why should I? Maybe I wasn't such a creep after all.

But two minutes later I very nearly ran away again. A girl driving by in a stubby green car yelled, "Hop in, Jen!"

Jen called out, "No, thanks, Carol!" and waved the car away.

A few others girls, one or two of them cheerleaders I recognized from pictures in the school paper, called Jen from across the street to join them. Jen shook her head, yelled, "See you at lunch!" and slipped her arm through my arm, talking away to me as if we were two close friends having this serious private conversation. Crowds of kids near the school came into view. Pure terror, but I couldn't escape because Jen had me arm-in-arm.

So many new experiences hit me that day and the days that followed, it's hard to say this one or that one was significant. Mostly, it was *being* — not running anymore — *being* with Jen and Larry and Dolph and Wayne, meeting them, their friends. Feeling the friendship, the playfulness. Drinking up the voices, the smiles, the surprise of someone calling your name. Realizing that you are in the river and it's okay because your body floats without your having to do anything special, and it's nice.

Probably the biggest experience was the first Lakeside football game. Wayne picked us up in his father's plush black Cadillac and kept the boys laughing all the way to the football field with anecdotes about the various night spots where he'd gotten turned down for singing jobs.

We got to the game early, so Wayne played his guitar while the stands around us slowly filled up with kids from school, and I tried not to leap out of my skin with nervousness. Wayne strummed and sang a new song lyric he was developing:

When our love is over
And life is empty time,
Will I still remember
Though we didn't have a dime
It was good, between us,
It was good.
California weather
When we are apart,
California weather
In my heart.

Wayne kept staring at me as if he were singing to me alone. Heads were twisted in our direction, but I desperately paid no attention. I happened to see one girl's face on a bench above us so jealous, and another girl yearning. Wayne winked at me and leaned toward me, as if we were in a spotlight. I suppose it was what you call a magic moment.

The actual game was a shock. A shock to be part of all the noise: the yelling and cheering when Lakeside scored, the anger and groans when Lakeside lost ground. I cringed seeing Dolph and Larry get knocked down so many times. But the crowd seemed to get a thrill out of all the smashing and crushing and crashing. The players played so brutally; Dolph particularly was almost murderous. And Larry directing the team seemed so stern. It bothered me. The only other person who seemed bothered was the Lakeside coach, Coach Bergman. He chewed his pipe, bit his nails, rubbed his bald skull, mashed his face into the palm of his hand.

What I liked best was the sight of Jen and the other cheerleaders leaping into the air, building a pyramid, doing acrobatics, whipping up the crowd to shout, "Go, Lakeside, Go!"

The rhythm of all the voices close around swept me along, and I couldn't resist shouting with them. With a long spinning pass from Larry to Dolph, Lakeside scored the winning touchdown. When Mark and Stevie ran out on the field to congratulate them, it gave me a queer feeling to see the two boys hoisted up on those huge shoulder pads of Larry and Dolph. Wayne knitted his fingers among my fingers and tugged me with him over to Jen. Jen, her face flushed, her eyes dancing, with lots of young men and women close around her talking all at once, singled me out and loudly said, "Maude, I'm so glad you came!" Some girls darted curious looks at me, as if they weren't sure what species I belonged to.

On the way home, Wayne talked a lot about how tough the music business is and how you have to be willing to live with empty pockets in crummy hotel rooms, etc. I wondered about him. Mark and Stevie tumbled out of the car and into our backyard.

Wayne leaned across the steering wheel toward me. "You're thinking about me, aren't you? Tell the truth!"

"I think you don't want to live in crummy hotel rooms."

A darkness stained his eyes and then a cocky grin chased the darkness out. "You're something," he said. "I'll pick you up at eight, Friday night."

My mouth went dry. "What?"

"Wear something sexy!"

"I . . . I . . . You . . ."

"I'm asking you for a date, Maude!"

I stepped out of the car. He winked at me through the window.

"Wait!" I cried.

"I will," he curved his lips, "but only until Friday!"

Dust flew around the exhaust of the black Cadillac. A moment later Wayne was gone.

I was afraid to start walking toward the house because my legs were suddenly so weak. My body sank down right on the patchy lawn grass. I had a *date*. With Wayne Grants. The first date in my life — unless I got run over by a garbage truck or slipped and drowned in the bathtub before Friday, which seemed eminently probable.

Images of Wayne kept falling through my thoughts like confetti. I did my chores in a trance state. I thought of a thousand reasons why Wayne would not show up on Friday. Friday was a million lightyears away. The earth might collide with a meteor.

Why hadn't I asked him where he was taking me? How should I dress? What time would we come back? Who was going to be there?

To make matters more complicated, Dolph cornered me coming out of school the next day and insisted on carrying my books. "Dolph, that's so old-fashioned," I whispered.

"Rightly so, that's how us cowpunchers like it," he said.

We had a pizza and soda. Then coffee and more pizza. He could *eat!* Dolph mentioned a paper he had to write for his class in Juvenile Justice. The subject was "Should teenagers have the right, if they die, to give away organs of their bodies to needy people?" I found my ideas coming out so easily, talking away and clicking my spoon in my coffee cup just like any other normal person. It was also peculiar that the minute Dolph got me talking, he completely erased my worrying about my date with Wayne.

So, by the time I got the phone call from Jen, my head was buzzing and my heart was delightfully confused with emotions about Dolph and Wayne and LIFE.

Jen's call was to say her typewriter didn't work, could she use mine. I almost chickened out, but I couldn't run away anymore. Yet I knew if she came over and spent hours with me, she'd find out for sure what an empty person I was. On the other hand, I was dying to tell somebody about Wayne asking for a date and Dolph buying me a pizza.

Jen came in the door with the sun shining behind her, making a golden halo out of the blond curls around her head. I marveled at the way her daring makeup highlighted the planes and curves of her face. She wore a pair of hip-hugging dungarees, and a cowboy shirt with bone buttons, and flashy green-and-blue striped sneakers.

"I really appreciate you letting me use your typewriter at the last minute, Maude." She swept past me into the house, smelling of orange blossoms. I must have had a grin from ear to ear, because she said, "What are you smiling at? Did I lose one of my eyelashes or something?"

She checked her eyelashes in the mirror. I couldn't believe someone like Jen could ever be bothered about eyelashes.

"I thought they were your real eyelashes," I said cautiously.

"Dear Mother Nature," Jen said, "needs a little help now and then. Take a look at these!"

She extended her long, smooth, perfect, gleaming fingernails. "My real fingernails look like they were attacked by your friendly neighborhood shark."

"I never saw you bite your nails."

"I'm a closet nail-biter," she clucked.

Wonderful, those hours in my house with Jen. We ate cold chicken and soda. She typed and talked at the same time. She showed me her new lipgloss and offered to try some on me, but I escaped to get more soda. She said funny things that made me laugh. The letters she typed were asking different colleges for applications. We ate leftover jello and asparagus. I didn't think until later that I didn't have anything interesting to say to her. Jen just seemed delighted to have me listen and ask a question or two. We ate chocolate pudding and yogurt.

There was only one bad moment. "You've *got* to go to college!" She flamed at me when she found out I was planning to attend a secretarial school. "That's ridiculous!"

But she wasn't really angry at me; she just cared what I did. Sometimes her tone of voice intimidated me, but most of the time her energy just swept me along. I almost started gushing to her about the date with Wayne coming up and my pizza with Dolph, but I thought she'd think I was silly.

Something had happened to me after I ran away from Jen on the street and then found that she still wanted to be my friend — a good thing. Other good things were happening every day. But still I was afraid: the more I got involved, the more I could be hurt.

And I was still capable of disaster. In the school cafeteria. Me with a plateful of mashed potatoes and gravy. Larry, alone at a table, waving me to join him. His sandy hair so charming over his forehead. The way he smiled was very different from Wayne and Dolph. Larry's smile was harder to figure out, as if there were always a question in his blue eyes.

I was so interested in the way Larry smiled and I was so engrossed in smiling back that I tripped and dumped my mashed potatoes and gravy on his shirt. He sat there hypnotized. I stared helplessly down at the mountain of mashed potatoes as it went sliding into his lap.

"My lap was so lonely until it found your mashed potatoes," he said.

Seven

Jen

"Should I kiss her on the first date?"

"No!"

There were boxes of shoes on the carpet around us in the middle of the shoestore, suede boots, hush-puppies, earth shoes, canvas tops, ripple-soles, each of which Wayne was on the verge of buying, and I thought any moment the sickly grin on the salesman's bloodhound face would shatter into pieces.

"I want shoes that make me feel ten feet tall," Wayne said. Then, heart-to-heart to the salesman, "And at the same time keep me connected to the earth."

The salesman touched his fingertips to his forehead, probably torn between *hara-kiri* and justifiable homicide.

While Wayne paraded up and down in front of the floor mirrors, the salesman, shaking his head, disappeared into the stockroom for a pair of desert boots.

"What do you think of the suede?" Wayne asked me.

"Suede is perfect for you. Suede shoes,

suede pants, suede pajamas, a suede tooth-brush, suede breakfast cereal — "

"Are you ticked off at me?"

"Oh, no, Wayne, I always love to watch shoe salesmen driven insane. And in case you didn't hear me, I *don't* think you should kiss Maude on the first date!"

Wayne rubbed his thumb greedily along the toe of a snakeskin boot, eighty dollars, on display. He hollered, "Could you also bring out a pair of the snakeskin boots, sir?"

Then, to me, Wayne breathed, "Jen, would you want me to kiss you on our first date, maybe the first date in your life?"

"We need to do what's good for Maude, not for me."

"I think I'll kiss her. Wayne Grants, organically grown kisses, no artificial ingredients. On the other hand, I've been told my kisses are habit-forming. Maude might become addicted. She might overdose! I wish I didn't have such an effect on women."

"One of these days your ego is going to get run over and there won't be an ambulance big enough to carry it!"

His manner switched to deadly serious. "I'm not fooling around on this Maude business!"

Then he switched again and saluted me slyly. "Chief, I'm going to make her feel like a million. I'm determined to make the world a better place! Can't you hear the lyrics?

One kiss for Maude
A lonely girl,

Will make the world
A better place to live i-i-i-i-i-n!

"You sarcastic rat!" He got me so mad I
hurled a shoebox at him, which missed, went
flying over Wayne's shoulder, and ricocheted
off the salesman's shoulder as he appeared
from the stockroom.

The salesman touched his forehead in disbelief and slowly surveyed the sea of shoes.
"I've been waiting for a moment like this to
give me the strength!"

The salesman smiled sweetly at Wayne
and me and he actually said, "Thanks!" and
walked right out the front door, whistling
gloriously. The store's boss, who'd been
watching us in a state of semi-paralysis, ran
to the street and yelled threateningly, "Winkler! Come back here!"

But Winkler grinned and waved and kept
on walking.

"Man, that poor dude, buried in shoes all
these years," Wayne brooded. "I could get
buried in my father's belt factory."

"Listen, you're going to be a big star, remember? You're a bit of a nerd, but I think
you're great to help Maude and risk a lot of
jerky kids bad-mouthing you."

Wayne perked up visibly. "I'll probably be
the first guy who ever kissed her. That first
kiss is a big responsibility!"

I stared at him suspiciously. "The girl is
completely inexperienced, Wayne. What
kind of kiss are you talking about?"

Without any warning, he gripped my

shoulders and slid his mouth over my mouth and I was so surprised I didn't push away or even tighten up, and my heart started racing so fast I couldn't talk for a moment when the kiss ended.

"This is not the balcony of your local movie theater!" the roly-poly manager grunted at us.

Wayne eyed the manager haughtily and we walked out.

On the sidewalk I snapped, "Don't ever do that again!"

"What?"

"Kiss me that way! I didn't like it."

"That wasn't my impression, Jen."

"I happen to love *Larry*, who happens to be your very close friend!"

"Sure, but if he's not making you happy — "

"I'm happy! Larry makes me very happy! If you knew the least little bit about being happy, you'd know you're looking at one of the happiest people you'll ever meet!"

"Okay, fine, I'll concentrate my new mind-bending laser kisses on Maude Harris and — and girls like *that* one!" He stabbed a finger at a lovely blond girl in the crosswalk.

I didn't stick around to watch Wayne try to pick her up, but I worried like crazy about what he was capable of trying with Maude, and I was especially unhappy because Wayne's kissing me shouldn't have hyped up my blood pressure the way it did. I guess it was natural to go running to Larry for reassurance.

We met in the park opposite my house. We walked along a path among high trees, and Wayne's kissing me in the shoestore only distracted me once or twice. I slipped my arms around Larry and pressed my face into his chest.

He lifted my chin, kissed the tip of my nose, my eyes, my mouth. I felt weirdly disloyal because my heart didn't react the way it had when Wayne kissed me, but no matter how exciting Wayne's kiss had been it couldn't change my feelings for Larry. I'd never take the chance of getting hooked on a Don Juan type like Wayne, who had more phone numbers than probably the whole telephone company, and I definitely intended to keep some psychological barbed wire between him and me.

Walking home, hand-in-hand and grabbing quick little kisses, I thought back over the afternoon and I marveled again at how my moods and feelings could swing so fast from way up to worse than down. The sun wasn't gone yet, not completely, you could see only one faint bluish star near the vanilla half moon, and Larry talked about how he wanted to study psychology when he went to college, except that my father had told him how tough it was for a psychologist to make the kind of money Larry could easily earn as something like a stockbroker or a corporate lawyer. Larry had this tremendous gift for sizing up situations and making quick, accurate decisions; he could, when he wanted to, convince a hippo it could fly.

The lights were on in my house, but Larry and I didn't go inside right away, owing to the fact that I was seething. I wasn't seething because of Larry but because of my father's trying to talk Larry out of being a middle-income but happy psychologist and into being a high-income but probably neurotic something else. Why are grown-ups always trying to talk you into making the same smart moves they made that made them so basically miserable?

"Let's never be unhappy, okay?" I whispered.

"Sure."

"Promise?"

"Cross my heart."

His voice sounded very deep and mature, the way it does sometimes when I least expect it, like he was suddenly thirty years old instead of eighteen. I pressed my cheek against his shoulder.

"People have so many problems, Larry."

"Not us."

"I bet Maude would open up more if she knew we had problems too."

"No more Maude now."

"It could make her feel important, to hear our problems."

"I don't have any problems," he said sourly.

"Tell Maude *your* problems."

"I don't have any either."

I reached up as if to kiss him and bit him hard on the nose instead.

Eight

Maude

Friday afternoon. Five hours before Wayne was coming to pick me up for our date.

A discount drugstore. Thousands of beauty products stared me in the eye. Dozens of soaps and shampoos and hair conditioners. How do you decide? My eyes jumped back and forth among endless brands of anti-perspirant. Countless face creams. Bath bubbles, after-bath splashes. One long wall of shelves crammed with lipsticks, like Hot Peach and Icy Rose, promising to make you someone who leaves men spellbound!

I was so bewildered I almost ran. Then I saw the cashier watching me. Recklessly, I snatched at bottles, tubes, jars, convinced that every choice was doomed.

I also bought my first pair of high-heeled shoes.

At home I sneaked up into my room and emptied two shopping bags over my bed-spread. The cosmetics terrified me. I could decorate a carrot cake but not my own face. I tore through the pages of several glamour magazines I'd bought and found the how-to-do-it articles. Okay, what can I practice on?

"Stevie-e-e-e-e-e? Stevie!"

Mark was working in splendid isolation on his Leggo construction. I got Stevie alone and said, "I'll give you a dollar if you let me practice on you."

"A dollar? I can buy pizza! *Practice what?*"

When he heard what I meant to do, the price tripled.

For two hours Stevie sat on a chair in my room with the door locked. I smeared lipstick on his lips, wiped it off, and tried again and again. He whined and moaned, as face powder, eyelash curler, eyeliner, eye shadow, eye powder, mascara, even false eyelashes went on and off and on and off with Vaseline, face cream, soap, and hot, wet cloths. Then he got so angry he punched a plastic bottle across the room. I paid him three very old worn dollar bills and let him go.

Racked with doubts, I locked the door. Then I heard Dad heavy on the stairs. He knocked and talked through the door.

"Getting ready for your date, Maude?"

"I will, Dad."

"You don't want to keep the boy waiting."

"I won't."

"What's his name again?"

"Wayne. Wayne Grants."

"I bought potato chips and soda in case the two of you are talking a lot and get hungry."

65

"Thanks, Dad."

"You tell him I said you have to be home by eleven o'clock."

"Whatever you say, Dad."

"Okay, how about midnight?"

"That sounds fine, Dad."

"Uh . . . we better make it no later than twelve-thirty."

I heard Dad's footsteps go downstairs.

Steam swirling around the bathroom, I took a shower hot as I could stand it. I'd bought three shampoos I couldn't decide among: Happy Hair, Gift from the Sea, Magic Cloud. I spilled a little of all three in my palm and lathered my hair into a heap of foam. Finally, I rubbed my skin dry with a rough towel, every inch of me. I wished I could rub off the years and years of running away from other people.

I wiped the mirror clean and evaluated myself. No change, the same dull Maude, except for a little something in my eyes. Odd, to examine your own face and find something new, or think you do. My eyes were — different. They had a — a what? A gleam of mischief maybe? A little perkiness? I couldn't help smiling at myself. Wayne Grants was coming to pick *me* up!

But I couldn't decide which set of makeup instructions to follow: the three-step, the six-step, or the nine-step. After twenty minutes of suffering, I picked a few steps from each and went to work on my face: face powder, lip-gloss, red pencil, black pencil, mascara comb, eyebrow brush, silver-gray eye shadow, snowflake-silver eyeliner, genuine false eyelashes made from the finest human hair, and to top it all off pink passion fingernail polish.

Casually, I edged into the living room. Mark saw me. His face crunched up ghastly as if he was watching a horror movie. Stevie stared at me and howled, "Daddy! Daddy!" My father turned with a big smile that vanished instantly.

"Maude! What did you do to yourself?"

I cried for a half hour in the bathroom while I scrubbed off every last touch of makeup. Almost made my skin bleed. Even scraped off the fingernail polish.

But I still thought at least I would try my new high-heels.

I needed to try *something* to surprise Wayne. I associated high-heels with glamour. But I wobbled so badly in them. For a while I practiced walking up and down my room. Then I heard the car, the doorbell, Wayne. Dad took Wayne in the backyard; the two of them were soon eating potato chips, while Mark and Stevie had a naval battle in a water-filled rubber pool. I nearly broke my neck coming down the steps in my high-heels and out the back door into the yard. I liked the sound the heels made clicking across the flagstones toward Wayne. Then one of my heels sank into the grass. I toppled sideways and came up choking in the rubber pool between Mark's aircraft carrier and Stevie's submarine.

Wayne was very understanding.

We missed the first ten minutes of the

movie. Kids from school were there, but Wayne kept his attention on me.

"Fabulous flick!" Wayne took my arm, leaving the movie, and waved to some friends.

I liked watching him talk, his mouth and eyes especially. In the car he raved about different movies and songs and new entertainers. His face was fascinating.

"What are you looking at?" Wayne opened the car door.

"Your face," I said without thinking.

He turned the key, the engine hummed. "What about my face?"

"It's beautiful."

Was he embarrassed? I couldn't imagine myself saying something that would embarrass Wayne. He drove us to an ice cream place called Peppermint Park. We shared a banana split. He told me about his career as a singer. "So far it's more a noncareer," he said.

More kids from school saw us. I still felt jumpy but I also felt the edges of satisfaction. A few times Wayne fidgeted uncomfortably when the conversation, which was mainly his, petered out.

"I'm out of conversation," he apologized.

"That's good."

"It is?" He relaxed.

Then, outside Peppermint Park, Wayne put the big car in motion to take me home, but the tires began bumping up and down. "Oh, no, a flat!" When we got out and looked, the car had two flat tires: one in front, one in the rear, on opposite sides. "I'm cursed!" Wayne groaned. "I've only got one spare!"

Who should come riding by just as Wayne was looking for a phone to call a garage but Dolph. Dolph on a bicycle and wearing a ten-gallon cowboy hat. Dolph insisted on taking me home, because it might be hours before Wayne got a tow.

"Sure," Wayne grumbled. "I'll have a ball out here all alone with my guitar and two flat tires!"

It was twelve-thirty, so I let Dolph sit me on the crossbar of his bike and we shot suddenly downhill away from Wayne, who called after us: "Go ahead, desert a sinking ship!"

The wind was whipping around us. Going so suddenly from Wayne to Dolph confused me. It also exhilarated me. Dolph's cheek touched my hair when the bike hit a pothole. His arms and chest were touching me. Dolph was another world from Wayne. Thrilling, but not so much in a physical way. The thrill with Dolph was more doing something daring with a friend. Then Dolph did something which almost made me fall off the bike. He kissed the back of my neck.

My father was a totally confused man when I arrived home on a bike instead of a car and with Dolph instead of Wayne. Dad made a real effort to seem very relaxed about it, until Dolph went to the bathroom. Then Dad whispered furiously, "That's not the same boy who took you out, is he?"

Dolph and I sat on the grass in the backyard. Inside, Dad watched television. There was quietness in the stars and faraway lights on the foothills east of the golf course. Linda pranced, flapped her tail. Dolph touched and talked to her as if she were a human being. I was remembering how it was on the bicycle when he kissed the back of my neck.

"Them there stars shore are plumb pretty, I reckon."

I smiled.

"I reckon my cowboy talk gives you a tickle. Mebbe you figger I ought to talk like all them tenderfoot city slickers."

I laughed.

"You got a hankerin' to know why I don't talk like other hombres?"

I shook my head.

"Good. It's a secret anyway, between me and them stars."

I wanted to put my hand over Dolph's hand, but I didn't have the nerve. "I'm glad you have a secret, Dolph."

He squinted at me as if he couldn't figure me out.

Then a familiar voice came out of the darkness. "Well, well, well, isn't this cozy!" It was Wayne. He'd climbed the fence. "My tires weren't flat at all. Some joker let the air out of them. Joker by the name of Dolph Krager!"

"Brother Wayne" — Dolph offered his hand to shake — "you sure as shootin' can take a joke."

"Thank you, brother Dolph. Now please

get on your cotton-pickin' lil' ol' mustang an' mosey on home. Maude is *my* date."

Dolph waved good-bye and disappeared.

"Why did Dolph let the air out of your tires?"

"I guess he likes you. Did he ask you for a date, the creep?"

"No."

Dolph came running back in that light-footed way he used on the football field. "Maude, can I take you bowling Sunday night?"

Overwhelmed, I nodded.

"I'm right honored, ma'am." Dolph bowed and dashed away again.

Grumpily, Wayne commented, "I think he's overdoing it."

A window slid open on the first floor and my father stuck his head out. "Getting a little late, folks."

"Sure, Mr. Harris," Wayne said agreeably.

"Hey, you're not the guy who brought her home!" Dad snapped. "You're the guy who took her *out*! What happened to the guy who took her home? No, forget it! I don't want to know!"

Dad's window slammed shut.

"Are you in trouble?" Wayne asked.

"I'm not sure," I said.

It was lovely thinking I might get in trouble because of a date. The best first date a girl ever had.

My life was heading somewhere new, destination unknown. I didn't know whether to laugh or cry. Jen, Larry, Dolph, Wayne — they were never out of my thoughts.

I'd go to sleep with a sweet, almost aching feeling right under my heart. I'd wake up with the fear that it had all been taken away from me, or was all a dream, unreal. I couldn't believe that two boys like Dolph and Wayne could want to be with me, take me out on dates, introduce me around. It couldn't be a joke or a trick because why would they waste their time with me week after week? And the same for Jen and Larry. I was forced to believe there was something in me they truly liked, something different, something my own.

The way my brothers and my father were changing toward me was *definitely* real. The boys seemed without doubt more careful around me and sometimes even polite, especially after Larry and Jen or Dolph or Wayne visited us. Mark and Stevie asked me endless questions about Dolph, Larry, and Wayne — I thought I noticed a new hint of respect in their voices. I even overheard Mark boasting to a next-door schoolmate: "We're gonna see *every* game. *My* sister is best friends with the star quarterback and the star runner!" My father seemed jovial and definitely more interested in me and kept slipping me money.

I also heard an unmistakable note of pride creep into my father's voice on the phone with his sister, long distance, one night: "I have to go now, Sarah, Maude's friends are coming over for dinner." I was glad my family seemed happier with me, but also troubled. How would they react if Jen and the others got tired of my company and dropped me?

But I didn't dwell on that possibility, because an exciting world was opening for me in school. I was surprised to find I had things to say that people would listen to. Every day my head was spinning with all the new kids I was getting to know. I couldn't remember half their names. There were friends of Jen, dozens; Wayne's musician friends; Dolph's friends *everywhere* — the bicycle shop, the bowling alley, the Pizza Palace, even the zoo where he knew one of the keepers.

Of the four of them, Larry introduced me to the fewest new people. The times I was with Larry without Jen, it seemed that most of his joking disappeared. He told me fascinating stories about animal behavior and mental illness. He showed me the animal lab. I didn't like the smell in the lab, where I saw monkeys who had an artificial mother made of wire and others who had an artificial mother of soft fur to cling to. The monkeys with wire mothers became much more neurotic, according to Larry.

"Makes you think about your own mother, doesn't it?" Larry asked. "Like, is she wire or is she fur?"

He spoke casually, but I was aware that he was pressing for an answer.

"It's complicated," I said.

"Why?"

"I don't remember my real mother, but I think she was probably wire. Then Nancy — she adopted me — she was really kind."

"I'm sorry."

"Why are you sorry?"

Larry had a way of flicking the soft sandy hair away from his eyes, but the hair would always fall down again over his forehead. "Asking you so many personal questions."

"I don't mind, Larry."

"I think you do."

He must have realized I was feeling bullied by him, because then he added, "Maybe I've been reading too many psych books."

"Sometimes you do sound like the school guidance counselor."

"Ouch! That hurts, Maude!" He grinned a crooked grin.

Day by day I developed a different way of looking at people. I started enjoying people's attention. Jealousy even crept in. Jealousy of other people getting attention from Jen or the guys. I even began depending on seeing them every day.

There were other changes too. The Bianchi sisters sat next to me in the lunchroom a couple of times and didn't stop talking for forty minutes about Dolph and Wayne. Gail Roddy borrowed some three-holed paper in study hall and whispered, "Isn't English boring?" Carol Duarte waved hello whenever she saw me and asked if I'd like to help out the prom committee. Mindy Schwartz honored me by reading aloud her as yet unpublished gossip column for the *Lakeside High*

Times, including a squib about me: "Who is the girl of mystery? Tall tales and scuttle-butt are making the rounds about one of our senior girls who has been posing for years as a hermit, but in fact beneath her everyday disguise there lurks a fascinating seductress. Her initials are M.H., in case you didn't know."

One day I invited Jen to come for a climb with me up Miller's Hill. My heart was hammering jittery, jumpy when I telephoned her, the first time I'd ever invited anyone anywhere. When she said yes I flew apart with pleasure.

To anyone else, probably, inviting a friend somewhere would seem easy. To me it was like walking on hot coals.

Miller's Hill was a few miles south of town. Jen and I were breathing hard when we climbed the last few yards to the top. "Fantastic view!" Jen said.

"You really like it?"

"Maude, I'm so glad you asked me to come." Her face glowed.

Off to one side was a very old graveyard still kept up by the county for historical interest. Names and dates on the old head-stones had been worn away by wind and rain. Jen abruptly turned her back on the graves. Her eyes flicked enthusiastically over the view of the town, the lake, farms, rail-road, the distant Cold Springs River. But the sight of the gravestones had dampened her spirits.

There was so much I wanted to say to her.

No one but Nancy had ever reached out to me like Jen. I wanted to say how grateful I was but couldn't. She might hate me sounding mushy and sentimental. Now and then I had noticed a lonely, restless look in her eyes. Did she need me too?

"Dead people are the pits!" Jen indicated the graves.

"I'm sorry I brought you here."

"No, no, no! I'm glad. It's just the graves I hate. Dying is so depressing."

"I saw my mother die. She was peaceful. She told me I never had to be afraid of dying."

We sat in silence for a while and then I said softly: "I always wanted one true friend to come into my life. And she did. *You* did, Jen."

It took a long time for Jen to answer me, as if something was stuck in her throat and she was having trouble swallowing.

"Thanks," she said in a very small voice.

"And . . . and I want to ask you to . . . to . . . to help me."

"How?"

"Please don't laugh when I tell you."

"I won't. I promise."

"Jen, you know so much about makeup and hairstyles and beauty and clothing. Maybe you can make me . . . different."

"Glamorous, Maude? Do you want to be glamorous?"

"I don't think it's possible. Do you?"

"I've been waiting for you to ask."

Nine

Jen

Hiking up Miller's Hill with Maude was the longest time I had ever been totally silent with anyone — climbing over rocks, giving each other a hand up now and then, grabbing a bush to pull yourself over a rough incline, seeing the flicker of joy in Maude's eyes when she pointed out an unusual bird or flower or spider's web. I was surprised at how uncomfortable it was not talking, and every time I was about to launch into some dynamite remarks I stopped myself, stubbornly, not wanting to be the first to break the silence. It's a lot like when looking into someone else's eyes gets so uncomfortable, but you don't want to be the first one to look away. Also, lately, around Maude, I'd been trying to cut out my jokes and smart remarks because I'd noticed they often made her flinch and wince, so there was even less to say than usual.

But then, little by little, the silence eased into a nice, laid-back, mellow attitude, in spite of the straining and sweating — a kind of peaceful space in my head — Maude and I grinning at each other, edging up the face of a tricky rock without much foothold. I wondered if Larry and I could ever be together without all the yakking, no pressure to be anything special, without *expecting* so much from each other.

A hundred yards or so from the top of the hill and leaning against the thick, rough trunk of a pine tree, I felt the shade of the branches like a huge, cool hand, and Maude and I seemed to be totally on the same wavelength until she said softly and hesitantly, "I think trees have consciousness."

She staggered me with that remark, because consciousness just isn't the kind of thing my friends talked about, but it seemed right on to hear Maude say it, because she sure knew how to be silent, just like the trees are silent. A little later, at the top of the hill, she startled me again the way she talked so simply about her foster mother dying. Not quite the kind of thing you would quote in Mindy Schwartz's gossip column.

Maude also scared me, because I realized how incredibly sensitive she was, and how unusual and intelligent. I felt a sharp pang of fear that the whole Love Experiment was liable to turn out horribly for her, even though that night my mind kept juggling different ways to create the "new Maude."

At breakfast the next morning my parents dropped a few little polite hand grenades about my spending all my time with a nobody like Maude and neglecting a fabulous guy like Larry with a 24-karat future. I stormed out of the room, angry at them and even angry at Larry, because they seemed to like him a lot more than they liked me.

Normally Larry should have been the first person I asked about dropping the experiment, but after that jazz with my parents I left his opinion for last, as if to pay him back for being so admired by my folks.

My fear of the experiment's hurting Maude had grown very real and I didn't want to be the guilty party, so I got hold of Dolph first and then Wayne, figuring they would be sure to agree with me because they were getting a lot of static in school by running after Maude. Sure, they were handling it in a very mellow way, but their friendly competition for dates with the least popular girl in Lakeside history made them perfect targets for anybody with a wisecrack at his fingertips. The way Dolph and Wayne played their parts you could see people beginning to think Maude must have a secret hyper-funky attraction, for two such dynamite guys to stand up to so much kidding.

Surprise, surprise. Dolph told me I was dead wrong about the experiment ever damaging Maude and that Maude could listen better than anybody he'd ever met. She really took his mind off how depressed he got.

Wayne, on the other hand, was suspicious when I asked him. He struck a wrong chord on his guitar. "What have you got up your sleeve, girl? What is this web you would weave, girl? Doodoo-doodoo-deedee-dadadoo-da!"

"*You*," I sizzled, "are the only singer I know with athlete's foot of the brain!"

I almost changed my mind about going to Wayne's audition that night, but when the horn honked and I knew Maude would be with him I jumped in the back of his father's battleship with Larry and Dolph, all of us coming along for moral support. Maude, half-smiling, sat near the window in the front seat as if she wanted some space between herself and Wayne, which made me skeptical about what he had been up to. The tires squealed and we were on our way out of town to some joint none of us knew, where Wayne had a possible singing gig.

I reached out and squeezed Maude's hand in a hello and she squeezed back. Ever since Miller's Hill, there was a closer bond between us, and her eyes were different when she saw me, not so hidden. When she allowed herself to smile, the smile did something new and nice to her face.

What made the ride to Wayne's audition memorable was when Maude — believe it or not — took out a pack of superlong, filter-tip cigar-colored cigarettes and, after lighting half a dozen matches, succeeded at last in causing the tip of her cigarette to flame up, almost singeing her eyebrows. She acted as if we were supposed to think she'd been smoking cigarettes since kindergarten, except that she held the cigarette like her fingers were a pair of scissors about to decapitate it, choked all over the place, and coughed so hard the cigarette did a swan dive and burned a hole in Wayne's new pink silk pants and his skin a little, too. Wayne almost drove his father's beloved two tons of shiny black steel off the road and into the river.

As if that wasn't enough, when we finally found the dumb place where Wayne was supposed to audition, it was a cheap little bar-and-grill with a neon sign blinking "Wild Times — Entertainment — Dancing — Good Eats." It was painted a very distinctive but anemic green, the paint peeling off in places as if the walls had leprosy or at least trench mouth. Wayne wanted to junk the audition, but Larry persuaded him to find the manager. The manager proved to be a greasy guy who sucked a soda loudly while Wayne sang and then cut Wayne off in the middle of his song. "Sorry, kid, can't use ya!"

Driving home, Wayne was knotted up and hyper, spurting jokes about the manager and how crummy the place was, only you *knew* it was killing him inside. Dolph and Larry and I laughed at his jokes because we didn't know how to reach him. Maude didn't laugh, didn't say a word, yet the vibes coming from her seemed to soothe Wayne, who kept glancing at her and catching her eye and slowly unwinding.

There was an old Elvis Presley record on the jukebox at the Pizza Palace when Larry and I dropped off there to be alone, Elvis really bending his voice around the lyrics of "Hound Dog." I snuggled close to Larry, trying to push away all those decisions about Maude, decisions about college, pressure from my parents, money problems, trying to juggle too many things, and knowing they were about to come crashing down on my head.

"Relax," he said softly, "I'm not Count Dracula." He exposed his teeth. "See, no fangs!"

"It's not you, Larry, it's everything. Us. The future. My parents. Maude. Mostly Maude. I'm afraid, like a premonition, she could get really wrecked if she ever finds out it's just an experiment, or if we all go separate ways and leave her, or — "

"Haven't you seen the change in that girl? You've done a fantastic thing for her! It's just the beginning. We can't stop now!" He sounded so strong and so sure of himself that I let my doubts be swept away and closed my eyes, grateful for his arms around me.

"And I think we should . . . you and I . . . the two of us" — Larry wrinkled his brow and wrestled with his words — "we should have a, well, definite commitment. I mean, like engaged. As in, to be married." He took my hand and held it between his two hands.

Impulsively, I kissed him. "Oh, Larry, it terrifies me!"

"Are you saying yes, no, or maybe?"

"Why do we have to decide so soon?"

"I don't know why. Well, maybe I do. Talking to Maude. She was saying how wonderful you are. She has a way of listening that just gets me talking and thinking, and that was when I decided why wait?"

I should have been happy Maude helped Larry get the idea to ask me. But it gave me a queer feeling.

"Marriage is heavy, Larry. I love you but I need to think about it. You're asking me to give up my secret underground laboratory in the Alps, my army of computerized humanoid robots, my dream of outwitting every slot machine in Las Vegas."

A shadow crossed his face. A shadow crossed my heart.

Ten

Maude

"Let me see you laugh."

"Laugh at what?"

"Just laugh, Maude. You're too serious. Start laughing and don't stop."

"Jen, I can't."

"Yes, you can!"

Jen was right. I laughed like an idiot but I did laugh. Jen got infected, laughing with me, each of us igniting the other until we were roaring, convulsed, gasping, and finally flopping on our backs on the rug, breathless.

"Why did you do a dumb thing like smoking that coffin nail on the way to Wayne's audition?"

"I thought it was glamorous."

"Maude, there are plenty of good old phony things to do to be glamorous that won't make your lungs a coal mine!"

In the days that followed, Jen had no mercy. Lessons in walking, lessons in talking, sitting, standing up. How to flirt, what to talk about with boys. Lessons in makeup. Dance lessons — a pile of her favorite records; a thousand times I was ready to give up, but the music never stopped.

"Shake, wiggle, and follow your body!" Jen demanded.

I had to practice lifting one eyebrow. "To get control of your face," Jen explained. *And* having long dialogues with myself in the mirror. "Loosen up your tongue," she said.

She even took me down to the beach when no one was there and had me yell at the waves. I had never yelled at anyone in my life, at least not with my guts in it. I started very meekly. Then I caught fire and yelled from the soles of my feet and really got into it, so much so that I got dizzy, though my throat wasn't hoarse at all. The waves were nice and understanding; they listened but they didn't yell back.

The biggest shock was my face. Jen spent hours experimenting. A cream blusher along the cheekbone and up the temple, brown shadow on the eyelid as a base, then a soft turquoise eye color with a smear of beige gold highlighter, false eyelashes — and on the mouth, *my* mouth, a dramatic orchid color plus lipgloss. When I was at last allowed to see myself in the mirror, it wasn't a girl staring back at me from the mirror, it was a woman.

"How do I look?" My voice trembled. "The truth, Jen!"

"Don't you know? You look absolutely stunning."

Jen dragged me to one department store and boutique after another, buying dresses, sweaters, pants, blouses, shoes, even daring underwear.

"I'll never wear it," I swore.

"Yes you will," she said patiently.

My bank account, years of allowances I'd scrimped to save, vanished. Ah, but the way Jen sailed into a store with me in tow and roamed around grandly! My usual way of buying was to slip into a store unnoticed, avoid the salespeople, who always intimidated me, and hope to find something and get out with the least possible fuss. But Jen was determined to find the *perfect* high heels, the *perfect* form fitting Levis, the *perfect* costume jewelry, and no grumpy saleswoman or sarcastic salesman could stop her. It had to be what she called *ultra ultra*.

"Jen, I couldn't let people see me like this, it's too . . ."

Jen smiled and instructed me in applying perfume to all the right places with the tips of my fingers.

"Now," she said, "I'll pretend to be a boy trying to pick you up, and you be terrific and wonderful."

I couldn't help laughing. That was part of what felt so good to be around Jen, feeling free to laugh.

"Hey, foxy lady!" Jen swaggered, mimicking a young man. "How's about you join me for a ride in my chariot and we'll go scarf down some brain food at the Pizza Palace?"

"Gee, that sounds swell," I said nervously.

"No, Maude. You tell him you can't possibly go with him but you smile so he knows you want him to talk you into it."

"But you've already talked me into it."

Jen threw up her hands in mock despair and laughed. "Maude, you're so damned honest, I love you!"

My face burned, fire in my cheeks and up to the roots of my hair. That Jen liked me, honestly truly liked me, kept me trying.

"Now let me see you smile so the guy knows for sure you think he is Numero Uno."

I tried to smile right, but my face felt out of shape.

"I give you E for effort, Maude, but it looks like you're trying to swallow a salamander. Relax and try again."

"Jen, I'm telling you, the way you've got me looking and acting, I couldn't face the people who knew me the way I was. All this makeup, clothes, play acting — it's not the real me."

"Maude, you can be anything you want. All the glamour stuff is just encouragement, sort of, so you let go a little, kind of plug in and drop the old uptight Maude who goes around pressing her self-destruct button whenever people get too close."

"That hurts."

"It's true, isn't it, Maude?"

"Yes."

"I'd like to have one place — one person — I could always tell the nitty-gritty truth to." Jen's voice surprised me, sounding so much younger, uncertain.

"So would I, Jen."

"We could try — with each other."

"I'd like that."

I caught once again that odd restless look in Jen's eyes.

"Jen, can't you tell the truth to Larry?"

"No, not all, not yet, but . . . but it's . . . getting there."

What Jen called the final touch in all the work she was doing with me was a little ritual that took place in a jewelry store she knew, where a buxom lady who owned the shop chattered away, pressing a cork against my earlobe and piercing it. She squirted hydrogen peroxide into the hole and pushed a gold wire through. It gave me the sensation of being definitely marked and changed, as if there was no going back now.

"Now we are going to show the new you to the world!" Jen announced.

I panicked. "I'm not ready!" No one, not even my brothers or father, had seen me with Jen's makeup. I'd always made sure to scrub it off, because I figured that Dad and Mark and Stevie had enough trouble getting used to me as someone with exciting friends and a real life outside the house. But maybe the truth was I still didn't have the courage to show my new self even to my own family. Was I afraid they'd laugh at me all made up? The boys, yes. Not Dad, though. He would frown, deep grooves in his forehead. He didn't like girls loaded with makeup. I also didn't want to shake Dad up because I already felt guilty about the condition of the house. Doing the chores had always given me a feeling of being needed, but lately I'd been so busy with Jen that I'd been doing the *minimum* cleaning and cooking. Dad hadn't complained, but it was hanging over me just the same.

Jen, of course, kept pressing me to at least let my family, Dolph, Wayne, and Larry see the new miracle me. I kept refusing and getting more and more anxious about it, and one night I absolutely decided I couldn't go on with Jen's changes. It was too upsetting. I went out on the golf course with Linda and ran until I dropped. I lay there in the darkness with my face pressed into the sweet-smelling clipped grass. "I feel like I'm being torn apart," I breathed into the earth, "the *old* me, the *new* me!" Linda licked my cheek and flicked her tail.

I couldn't resist Jen's energy. She borrowed a car to drive me over to Southhope where nobody knew me. We did all the dressing and makeup at Jen's house and she hustled me into the car, wearing enormous dark glasses. In Southhope we walked down the main street together and nobody in particular stared at me. A few boys whistled, I presumed at Jen. Jen marched me in and out of half a dozen stores and gradually confidence oozed into me. I couldn't believe I passed my first test without once falling flat on my face. Well, I did drip my yogurt ice cream cone on my new dress, but Jen laughed and said, "That's an improvement. At least you're spilling it on yourself, not someone else."

The next day Jen insisted that I "solo." I was wearing a slit skirt and a filmy French blouse. We drove to Millville. Jen sat in the car while I walked through town by myself. It went fine except for one minor accident when two kids on bicycles, Mark's age, almost ran me down and I snagged my skirt on a wire fence.

I felt fairly self-confident until Jen informed me that the two of us were scheduled next for a dance, in public, granted where no one knew me — in Southhope — but a *dance!* Oh, no!

I was standing on the end of a diving board a hundred feet up and Jen was pushing me — "Dive! Dive!" — but I didn't see any water in the pool.

Eleven

Jen

Maybe I was pushing Maude too fast. Maybe Larry was pushing *me* too fast.

He came jogging toward me at football practice — a springy loping stride, graceful and confident — swipes of black grease on his cheekbones, shoulder pads bulging under his white jersey, a sleek gold-striped black helmet in his hand, and the wind hooked his hair, and he smiled so persuasively.

"What did your folks say about us getting married?"

"Haven't told them, O Divine One."

It dawned on him that I hadn't made my mind up, and his smile dissolved like a mud-ball in a malted.

"Larry, how can you be so sure it's the right thing for us?"

"Because, look at Wayne or Dolph, always crumming around for something they never find. Well, you and I, we've found each other, we go good together, we have fun, we enjoy each other, we might even learn to like each other." He laughed attractively at his own joke and went on. "So why take the risk of losing what we have?"

"You mean what we have is safe, money in the bank, a ticket on a train to a nice little town, and you can go on your business trips and I can have my committees. Larry, maybe safe isn't enough."

His lips narrowed and he smacked his helmet onto his head. "Safe is great because we love each other, you turkey!"

The coach's whistle blew and Larry bounced back toward the gridiron for a scrimmage, but wheeled around, cupping his hands over his mouth and shouting. "If you can't say yes by the end of the week, I'll figure you mean no!"

I could have choked him — giving me a deadline! Why couldn't we just go on the way we were? On the other hand, what was stopping me from saying yes?

What would Larry say about getting engaged if he knew that sometimes his funny, happy, energetic girl, Jen Robbins, was so confused and scared and just plain miserable that, looking at her face in a mirror, she hated the sight of it.

So I kept on with the Great Love Experiment, which seemed to have a momentum all its own and stopped me from thinking too much, though in the back of my mind I hoped a decision about Larry would just happen. A dozen times a day I thought Maude would give up smack in the middle of all my efforts, but I badgered her, and pleaded with her, and yelled at her, and laughed with her, and when she laughed for the first time with me she looked like magic was being done to her face. I wished Maude and I could be *real* real friends in the future when the experiment would be over. With each new thing we did, she became looser and more open, and her face slowly dropped a lot of tension and in its place a mysterious little smile would flicker about her mouth. Her eyes began to have a kind of subtle welcoming quality that made me wish I had some in *my* face.

Still, she resisted exposing herself in makeup and glamour duds to anyone but me. She wouldn't even step outside her room for fear her brothers might see her. Maude had gotten so used to being alone that she was able to accept herself that way and even get some goodies out of it. Secretly, I suppose I admired the way Maude had hung in by her lonesome, an outsider, and hadn't gotten moody or nasty or turned-off.

Being with Maude so much, basking not a little in her admiration, another thing happened: the idea was planted in me that maybe someday I might want to live all alone for a while, on a beach or in the woods, and introduce myself to myself and see how we'd get along, but I wouldn't try it until I was very old.

The problem was still to give Maude enough confidence to face people with her new face and new etcetera, so I decided she might gain some belief in herself if we went to a dance — again at Southhope where no one knew us — and I only got her to go by swearing we'd leave the minute anyone laughed at her. To inject a little pizzazz into the night, I suggested we use false names and invented for her the name Carlotta Sutherland, and Maude picked for me the name Ingrid Barrymore. Well, the minute Carlotta Sutherland showed her face at that dance there were boys coming out of the woodwork to dance with her, which I took a little credit for, the hours I spent making the most of her hidden assets — hips, pelvis, neck, shoulders, legs, and a very modest but sort of Continental bust. Maude kept whirling away with different boys and did she blossom right in front of my eyes, like seeing a dry little weed suddenly perk up and shoot out bright green leaves and dazzling dark rose petals! I had my own admirers buzzing around, but she kept coming back to me for security, and I could hardly keep from laughing every time I heard those two names on our lips: "Hi, I'm Ingrid Barrymore! This is my friend, Carlotta Sutherland."

The only zilch happening at the South-hope dance was when this hotshot guy showed up — with millions of freckles, sunset red hair stabbing out in all directions, and fierce blueberry eyes — and started monopolizing all my dances. I got fed up with his waving away all the other guys who wanted to dance with me, although I did like his gravelly voice and that he didn't bother with small talk, but asked me weird, interesting questions that threw me off-guard. In spite of his conversation I didn't like his voltage and wanted to get him out of my hair, except you knew he was trouble galore if you pressed the wrong button on his ego. I didn't want anything to spoil Maude's good time, so I danced every dance with him. Sonny Goldhammer, he called himself, blue eyes poking at me and red hair catching the lights like a halo. Sonny Goldhammer absolutely did not *have* a halo. After the band played the last dance, Sonny wouldn't let me hustle Maude into my mother's station wagon until I had written down my name and phone number for him: Ingrid Barrymore, and a number as phony as my fingernails.

Getting rid of Sonny Goldhammer, I breathed easier, and it all seemed worthwhile when Maude agreed to my setting up a cookout for Sunday afternoon at Willis Park where her two brothers and her father, and Wayne and Dolph and Larry, and say a few select girls from school would gape and gasp at a Maude none of them would have believed possible. I had the idea also that come the Sunday cookout, I would somehow be inspired with an answer for Larry's proposal. Maude called me a dozen times for assurance that everything would go great, and the excitement gave me such a light-headedness that I thought maybe at last I was really getting my act together.

The only fly in the ointment was Wayne, who was mucho depressed over not getting any singing gigs and came with me to buy charcoal a few days before the cookout. He gloomed all over me. "I think I'll kill myself probably, Jen. Anybody ever commit suicide by taking an overdose of Ovaltine?"

"Maybe you ought to marry a rich older woman, somewhere in her mid to late millions."

"Jen, I'm serious! Maybe if I had someone like you to stabilize me, I could make it as a singer."

"Wayne, you couldn't stick with one girl unless her skin was made of Elmer's glue."

"Oh, yeah? I haven't dated anyone but Maude for weeks and I'm surviving."

"Well, maybe *Maude* can stabilize you. I have to admit you make it look plenty genuine the way you go after her."

Sullen, Wayne hoisted the big bag of charcoal and carried it out to throw in the back of my mother's station wagon. "The only reason I turn to Maude is because I'm mad about *you*." With his hands freed of the charcoal, he suddenly grabbed my arms. "Jen, my heart is a Boulder Dam, filling up with millions of gallons of love for you!"

"Let me go, you clown!"

"Jen, even a clown has feelings."

I stamped my heel on his foot and broke free of him.

"OW!" he howled. "My toe!"

"You're just lucky Larry doesn't know," I snapped, and slammed into my mother's car and left him flat.

I didn't see Wayne again until the picnic. His toe obviously had survived, judging from the way he danced around Maude all afternoon.

The dozen people at the picnic had never seen Maude without her tight braided hair, dumpy dresses, no makeup, etc. You never saw people drop their jaws and gape in amazement like they did when I purposely arrived late in my mother's station wagon, opened the door for Maude, and unveiled a creature who knocked everybody's eyes out.

Maude put her legs out of the car first, long white legs which had always been hidden under those clunky, baggy dresses. At the top of her legs now were a pair of purple velvet shorts, and the curves of her legs slimmed down to a pair of dynamite ankles. Her hair, freed from its usual tight braids, hung loose and shimmering to her shoulders. Her mouth was shaped with glossy lavender, and her eyes, when she languidly removed a pair of big dark glasses, had an Egyptian touch, like those pictures of Queen Nefertiti.

At first the reaction was total silence. Conversation stopped cold. Everyone couldn't have been more stupefied if they were watching someone rise from the dead.

Even I was surprised at how sexy Maude seemed. Something subtle had happened to her since the dance at Southhope. The way she carried herself, a sense of freedom in the way she moved her shoulders and hips, a certain daring in her expression — I felt like a magician who creates an illusion and then finds the illusion is doing its thing on its own.

Larry squeezed my arm, winked, and in a whisper told me I was a miracle-maker, which for some reason I didn't enjoy hearing. Dolph and Wayne put on their usual act of competing for Maude's company. Wayne obviously turned on for real, but with Dolph I couldn't tell. Maude's father appeared very cool about her new look, but he kept darting sideways glances at her as if she reminded him of someone he couldn't quite place. Mark and Stevie sort of shied away from Maude, awed by the change. Mindy, Carol, and Gail barraged me with whispered questions about Maude.

Amazingly, Maude seemed more at ease than I'd ever seen her. All afternoon, the males and the females of the species kept screwing up their eyes at her as if she were a mirage or something. Buttered corn steaming on the cob came and went, and so did dripping, juicy charcoal-broiled burgers and hot dogs, potato salad, garlic bread, blueberry pie, and ice cream. Maude didn't eat much, I noticed, maybe because she was too busy drinking in all the new admiration. The high point of the cookout was the touch football game when Dolph and Larry chose up sides. For the first part of the game Maude avoided the ball like it would bite her, but her team was losing and the other team threw the ball and she caught it almost by accident and Larry yelled, "Run, Maude! Don't just stand there!" Something clicked, and suddenly her legs were a blur and nobody could touch her.

Dolph tried to tag her but, compared with her, he looked like he was running in pea soup up to his knees while she was running on air. He chased her clear to the goal line and he looked pretty foolish.

"You are fantastic," Dolph wheezed at Maude, and clapped his arm around her shoulder. "You oughta try for the track team, the Olympics. You could beat anybody!"

Maude picked a speck of dirt off Dolph's chin and said very seriously, "Running is something I do alone. I'm not interested in being better than anybody else."

"Maude," Larry asked, "where did you learn to run like that?"

"I run at night."

"At night?"

"On the golf course."

"Naturally."

"With my dog Linda."

"That figures."

Larry looked at Maude with an expression on his face I couldn't decipher, sort of as if he were seeing her for the first time and didn't know quite who she was.

There was a quarter-moon that night when Larry and I were finally alone together on the beach. From where we sat on the cold sand we could see the dark and white curling waves rolling in and giving the beach soft slaps, and sometimes a thump, like a fist hitting an empty barrel. Way out on the water there were lights like fallen stars that meant a ship we couldn't see, and the clouds drifted across the quarter-moon like thin black scarves.

"Larry, I'd like to get engaged to you."

"Sorry, but I'll have to think about it for a millisecond or two."

He didn't get excited or even smile but he looked at me very seriously, and we took off our shoes and walked barefoot in the soft sand, where the waves going backward into the sea had left wide loops of foam.

Twelve

Maude

The air whipped against my face whenever I leaned my head to one side and looked at the black-topped road disappearing under the handlebars of the battered Kawasaki motorcycle Dolph had borrowed. I sat behind him with my arms wrapped around his waist, excited, scared, happy.

"Another fifty miles." His voice penetrated the roaring engine. My first motorcycle ride, the road vibrating into my body. So many firsts: my first girl and boy friends, first date, first high-heels, first dance, first (and last) cigarette.

Weeks ago Dolph had kissed my neck when I was riding on the crossbar of his bicycle, but he hadn't tried to kiss me again. Did I want him to? Maybe. Was I falling in love with him? I didn't think so.

Was I falling in love with anyone? I wanted to. I wanted to fall in love.

We hit a pothole. I tightened my grip around Dolph. He laughed. What I couldn't

understand about Dolph was that I could see
he was affected by my perfume and makeup
and clothes and all — the new sexy me —
yet he remained very sweet, attentive, took
me to the zoo twice, fishing twice, but never
tried to kiss my neck or me. It didn't make
sense that a boy would kiss your neck when
you looked like the old dull Maude Harris
had looked, and then when you start looking
sexy for the first time in your life, he doesn't
even give you a peck on the cheek.

The Kawasaki flew past tracts of look-alike
houses, gas stations, more houses, meadows,
tilled land, barns, farmhouses, orchards; and
my mind roamed back over the dance at
Southhope and the picnic, especially the picnic. I had cringed in the back of Jen's car in
those velvet shorts and then when she had
opened the door for me to step out, somehow
a force, a new strength had flowed into me.
Remembering the picnic, the way people's
eyes had come alive on me in ways I'd never
experienced before, gave me goose bumps.
Wayne's eyes had darted over me from head
to foot. The expression on Dolph's face had
been wide-open surprise and pleasure. Larry's reaction had been very enthusiastic, full
of compliments, yet keeping at a distance. I
was remembering my dad and brothers, that
night at home after the picnic. Almost in-
stinctively, Mark and Stevie had given me a
wide berth and stopped yelling *"Maude get
me this"* and *"Maude get me that"* all the
time. Dad was much more quiet than usual,
didn't ask me all the questions that were his

habit. And since the picnic, the voice of the house — houses have voices, too (for years the house had called me twenty times a day: do the bathroom, do the kitchen, the bedrooms, the rugs, tiles, woodwork, laundry, dust this, wash that, scrub, mop) — the voice of the house had lost its hold over me.

I recalled when the kids and teachers in school had seen me for the first time, a day after the picnic, in my stunning new clothes and makeup: a butterfly out of her cocoon. Some hadn't recognized me. Others looked struck dumb. Four boys asked for my phone number, and I said no but felt WOW! Jen had summed it up: "You have managed, my dear Carlotta, to warm the cockles of their eyeballs."

With my arms tight around Dolph on the Kawasaki, I tried to shake off the persistent memory of Dolph kissing my neck. I had never been kissed by a boy and I didn't know how other girls felt when boys looked at them, but ever since the picnic the way some boys stared made me feel giddy, champagne bubbles in my veins.

So when Dolph stopped to fill up at a dusty little gas station, I suddenly burst out: "Dolph, why did you kiss my neck?"

"Huh?"

"On your bicycle. My neck."

"My bicycle?"

"The night you let the air out of Wayne's tires. Why did you kiss my neck?"

"Did I kiss your neck?"

"Yes, you did," I said.

"You're right, I did. Why did I kiss your neck? You ask the damnedest questions, Maude! How do I know why I kissed your neck?" He sounded angry.

He paid for the gas and moodily swung his leg over the motorcycle. I climbed on behind him. We took off so fast, the rear wheel screamed. There was, I decided, a lot to learn about the mysteries of the male ego.

Dolph's mood lightened, however, as soon as the Kawasaki swung past a rough wooden fence and under a sign with burned-in letters: DOUBLE YOUR LUCK RANCH. Not much of a ranch, rambling wood fences, ramshackle farmhouse, barn tilted to one side, several small corrals with three or four horses nibbling grass. A short barrel-chested man with a bushy mustache stomped from the barn, whooped loudly, and lifted Dolph off his feet. A tall, fat lady wiping her hands on her apron came off the porch and pinched Dolph's cheek and kissed him.

Harvey and Laura Herrigel treated us like family. They had no children of their own. They both worked for the post office and planned to retire in a few months. They had named their little piece of land and half a dozen horses "Double Your Luck Ranch" because Harvey had grown up on a working ranch and dreamed of living that life again. Dolph had met them at a rodeo show.

"We got our eye on a real workin' ranch that might be up for sale real cheap," Harvey said, resting on the porch after lunch, and Dolph eagerly pressed him for more details.

I came away from Double Your Luck Ranch with so much to remember. Harvey and Laura, a way of life I'd only read about. Dolph gripped the handlebars of the Kawasaki, going home at half the speed we came, and said nothing until he pulled into an isolated road rest.

"You're the only one who knows about the Double Your Luck Ranch. Let's keep it that way!"

"Sure, Dolph."

"What did you think of Harvey and Laura?" Dolph asked.

"I think you love them!"

Later, opening the door of my house for me, Dolph said, "Maude, you're a lot of girl," and kissed my forehead.

Was I disappointed or delighted? Both. A kiss on your forehead, was that a step up or a step down from a kiss on your neck? Down, probably. When you've never even been kissed on the mouth by a boy, you're not quite sure what means what. I didn't think I wanted to fall in love with Dolph, but who knows? Still, a kiss was a kiss, and what with the zing of the motorcycle and the fun of Harvey and Laura's ranch, I was bubbly all over until I saw what awaited me in the kitchen.

Fingerprints on the refrigerator, peanut butter fingerprints, grape jelly fingerprints, and plain old dirt fingerprints. In the sink a jumble of pots, dishes, silverware, *Star Wars* drinking glasses, and a layer of reddish grease. A sock and a torn T-shirt hanging over the kitchen chairs. Scuff marks on the floor, plus enough assorted squashed bits of food to feed every ant in the neighborhood.

Sighing, I squeezed soap into the sink and twisted the hot water tap. Bubbles began to foam up. The happiness of the day began to dissolve. "No!" I said loudly and jerked the faucet closed. I wanted to lie in bed and relive the excitement of the motorcycle, the leather smell of Dolph's jacket, the air running over us, the ranch, the horses, the hills, the bigness of the sky.

"Let someone else clean up!" I muttered, taking the stairs to my bedroom two at a time.

Upstairs, on my desk, I found a mysterious note in Jen's flamboyant handwriting: "News flash! Please call me or I'll explode. You'll be the first to know. The heart is a lonely surfboard. Stop the world, I wanna get on! Jen."

While I dialed Jen's number, I found myself harboring suspicions: why would *I* be the first to know anything important about her? Didn't she have a dozen girl friends she'd tell before me?

Over the phone, Jen's voice sounded so brittle: "Maude, Larry and I are getting engaged! I demand that you come with us to buy the ring."

She paused, waiting for me to speak, but I was trying to imagine her as a housewife, and wondering.

"Well, my dear Carlotta" — she put too much effort into sounding lighthearted — "what do you think? Will Larry and I get married and live snappily ever after? Look in your crystal ball!" Then her voice deepened, a trifle hoarse: "Your opinion means a lot to me, Maude."

"Jen, I . . . I think you sound very uncertain."

There was a weighty silence at Jen's end of the line. I heard her sigh, "Thanks, Maude. I mean it. See you tomorrow."

Jen clicked off. I sat staring through my window at the rain dripping on the pine boughs and catching gleams from the street light. Did Jen take getting engaged seriously? It was hard to imagine her high spirits ever tied down. I'd heard girls in school talk boldly about how marriage wasn't any big deal because you could always get a divorce but I always felt people must get eaten away by a wrong marriage, and bouncing from one guy to another can't feel good.

The phone rang. It was Wayne. He wanted to take a walk. I told him it was eleven o'clock and my father was asleep. Wayne said he'd been walking the streets alone for hours and couldn't I slip out for a few minutes for a friend? He said his father was going to sell the belt factory and retire unless Wayne took a full-time interest in learning the business.

"He'll make me a partner and eventually I'll be president," Wayne groaned a few minutes later as we walked along the dark residential streets, leafy trees allowing only a lace of light to fall from the street lamps. "But I'll have to give up singing, except as a hobby."

"Is that so bad, Wayne?"

"Bad? I'll tell you how bad! How would you like to be a seagull with both your wings nailed to a desk all day for the best years of your life?"

I wanted to make him feel better so I took his arm and said, "I wish I could help."

"You can, Maude." He cupped my face in his hands. I knew he was going to kiss me. I didn't resist. And yet I didn't want him to be the first. His mouth touched my mouth. My lips were stiff. I recalled Jen's advice and tried to let my lips be pliant. But my eyes were shut tight. Then he kissed me in a way I had only read about. "Ever since I saw you in those purple hot pants at the picnic, I haven't stopped thinking about you. Maude, you're solid, but you're also pretty wild. Larry and Jen are getting engaged. Maybe that's what *we* should have in mind, Maude. You know, for the future."

His words sank in. My heart squeezed inside me. His white teeth, glossy curly hair, penetrating eyes, silky voice, had a powerful, almost hypnotic effect.

"I think you should stop dating Dolph or anyone else as of now, and you and I should be just for each other. You tell Dolph tomorrow."

"Wayne, I'm not . . . not sure."

"You will be," he said.

I sure needed advice about Wayne. Alone in my room I picked up the phone a dozen times to call Jen. But I hesitated. Maybe I needed advice from a boy. Maybe my image of Wayne as too slick and untrustworthy wasn't fair to him. I thought of Larry, his blue gray eyes, sandy hair. Larry would be good to talk to. I liked thinking about Larry more than anyone. That was hard to admit to myself. I felt terribly guilty, because Jen was my friend. But the more I tried to stop thinking about Larry, the more his honest, open face, his smile (sometimes challenging, sometimes mystifying), the little white scar on his forehead, his strong jaw, kept appearing in my mind.

I guess I'd been trying not to think about Larry since the day I first met him.

Was I falling in love with him? That would be a cruel thing to do to myself.

Thirteen

Jen

Nobody was seriously hurt during the fight that broke out at the Rainy River House the night Wayne tried to sing there, but it was black eyes and bloody noses galore, people socking people in the jaw, hiding under tables, throwing chairs and soda cans and hamburgers, bodies crashing through windows, and it opened my eyes to the fact that *my* Larry could possibly have eyes for someone else.

And who did I meet in the middle of that inane brawl but Sonny Goldhammer from Southhope, the same freckles, flame red hair, deadly blue eyes, and it was like fate was giving me a kick down a road I shouldn't travel.

The Rainy River House was a hangout for older high school kids from three different townships, a place so rowdy they actually frisked boys at the door. We'd never been there because Coach Bergman didn't want his team in fights, but it happened that

110

Wayne finally got his first paid professional singing gig there.

The very first bad twinges I had about Maude came the night of Wayne's debut.

Dolph and I were waiting at my house to be picked up by Larry and Maude. Dolph dropped himself into an armchair with a long sigh. "Pardner, my little ol' barn of a heart is just a-burstin' with congratulations for you and Larry. When you aimin' to have the engagement party?"

"Whenever Larry desires. Will you baby-sit for us someday and let our kids spit up on your T-shirt?"

Dolph snorted. "Amigo, you used to be a mite funnier."

"You don't look so funny yourself lately."

"I got halfway football offers from three colleges, but I don't know where I'm a-goin' or what I'm a-goin' to do when I get there. Not like ol' buckaroo Larry — he's got his future laid out like a railroad track."

"We might jump the tracks now and then," I said defensively.

"Mebbe so. You know, I've been thinking, if I had a bullet's worth of sense in my head I'd stick with someone like Maude the rest of my life, 'cause she is got to be the most honestest humanest real soul quality person I ever knew."

I forced a smile at Dolph, but I didn't have a smile in my thoughts, because his extravagant praise of Maude had twisted a knife in me that I hadn't known was there.

Larry brought Maude over in his Dad's old

pickup and the four of us headed out toward the Rainy River House, but passing a small lake Larry saw steam pouring from a white-haired old lady's car. When he and Dolph jumped out to help the old lady, Maude grabbed my sleeve and said, "Please, Jen, stay here, I have to talk to you."

So, while Larry and Dolph yanked open the hood of the white-haired lady's car, Maude proceeded to gurgle forth the latest installment in her life with Wayne Grants.

"And then he hinted we should get engaged."

"Did you believe him, Maude?"

"No."

"Then what's the problem? He obviously turns you on. Why not just enjoy it?" My voice sounded, even to me, kind of peppery unsympathetic.

"I don't want to be Wayne's girlfriend, not the way *he* has in mind, but I also don't want him to stop seeing me, because . . . because he makes me *feel* . . . a lot."

"I guess you have to give a little to get a little," I said in a dry voice, and immediately disliked myself for sounding so phony-sophisticated and for sort of enjoying Maude's dilemma.

But mostly I wanted to wring Wayne's neck for coming on to Maude with that engagement baloney, especially since we had all sworn not to do anything to hurt her, way back at the Cold Spring River campfire when the experiment began. On the other hand, I was sick and tired of Larry raving over

Maude's great listening ability and intelligence, Dolph glorifying her illustrious soul quality, and now Wayne hinting he might get engaged to her! It was a little much. I mean, after all!

Even when we were finally seated in the Rainy River House, jammed in with so many other people and tables the waiter could hardly reach you and facing a stage the size of a dartboard, I still wasn't sure whether to tell Larry about Wayne's crummy engagement ploy with Maude. Maude and Dolph were dancing to the jukebox before Wayne's first set, and I kept glancing at Larry and wondering acidly, "Do *you* also think Maude is the most real, honest, human quality person you ever met?"

That's when I blurted out all the details about Wayne coming on to Maude, because I was dying to see Larry's reaction. And react he did, quickly and bitterly, unlike him because he usually chewed things over before giving an opinion. "All the years I know Wayne and he turns out to be a rotten filthy creep!"

At that moment Wayne strode into the spotlight with his guitar, and the rowdy audience slowly quieted down when he struck the chords for a new song I'd never heard, by which time Maude and Dolph had snaked back to our table. Wayne gave out the lyrics in his sexiest lowdown voice, sending them straight to Maude and pouring it on as if he and she were the only ones there:

Knock knock knock, I'm knockin'!
Baby, can't you hear me call?
Rock rock rock, I'm rockin'!
Why you wanna see me crawl?
Ring ring ring, I'm ringin'!
Baby, won't you lift the phone?
Sing sing sing, I'm singin'!
Ooh, you got a heart of stone!

Larry saw the half-hypnotized, half-giddy, half-embarrassed look on Maude's face and suddenly smacked his fist down loud on our table before Wayne's song was finished, shouting at the top of his voice: "Boo! Boo! Get that bum off the stage! Get that stage out from under that bum!"

Three burly characters at the table in front of us told Larry to shut up. He indicated they should get lost. In a matter of seconds Dolph and Larry were diving into five or six guys at once. Wayne, though he'd seen Larry start the ruckus, settled his guitar gently behind a speaker and leaped feet first on some guy choking Larry from behind. I grabbed Maude to get out of there, but the entire place was erupting around us in all directions, and suddenly somebody was steering the two of us steadily toward an exit I hadn't noticed, and that somebody was absolutely Sonny Goldhammer.

When he got us outside the Rainy River House you could still hear things smashing inside and a faraway police siren. Maude and I both began shaking because we really had come close to getting our hairdos busted open, so we didn't resist when Sonny shoved us inside a sleek white car that had a high rear end, road-scraping front end, and furious red painted flames sweeping from the headlights to the rear bumper.

Sonny's car rammed out of the parking lot and into the road, whipping past a police car's flashing red light, zooming ahead of a truck that was hogging the road, skidding a couple of bad curves, and narrowly missing an oncoming car whose headlights washed our faces; and I thought this is the first and last time I ever ride with Sonny Goldhammer, but I was too grateful about getting out of the brawl to complain about his driving.

Sonny must have read my mind, because he said, "Sorry, Ingrid, I'll slow down, as a favor to you and Carlotta."

"Sonny, I want to apologize. Those aren't our real names."

He chuckled. "Ingrid Barrymore! You know I telephoned every Barrymore within a hundred miles of Southhope? I bet your real name is Esmerelda Crump!"

"Jen Robbins," I said humbly. "Esmerelda Crump is my stage name."

When Sonny's brakes squealed to a stop in front of my house, I knew I'd have trouble getting rid of him. Maude and I got out. She actually caught Sonny's hand and shook it hard, something I never taught her. Sonny grinned at me mischievously: "Jen, you owe me at least one date."

Standing at the door of his white car, one arm on top of the painted flames, his fist cocked on his hip, a laid-back look on his freckled face, he reminded me of a rooster ready to crow, and I resented the way he seemed to think he was irresistible.

"I can't date you, Sonny. I'm getting engaged."

"Have you done enough comparison shopping?" he twinkled, sliding into the driver's seat and slapping the door shut. "See you! Watch out for the ball and chain! So long, Maude!"

Watching his white bomb flash away under the street lights, I fumed, "So pompous!"

My mom's car was in the driveway so I borrowed it to drive Maude home. Maude was worried about Dolph and Wayne and Larry. I told her not to be a dope because the guys knew how to take care of themselves and didn't like girls to make a big fuss about a fight. I guess I sounded pretty arrogant, but Maude didn't seem to mind and even pressed my hand when she got out. I had to keep fighting off this feeling of being annoyed at Maude for no real reason. One minute I was grateful to have become her friend, even in so artificial a way as the Love Experiment was, because with her I was starting to understand what a real friend felt like. The next minute I was back being more than a little fed up with the way Dolph and Larry and Wayne kept talking about how Maude *listens* and she's *deep* and all those beautiful *quiet* qualities that I, Jen, had been short-changed of.

116

At home, when I telephoned Larry's house, nobody answered and I remembered his father worked nights and then Larry opened my front door, pretty beat up. I cleaned his cuts and didn't cross-examine him or say anything nasty about how dumb I thought it had been for him to start banging on the table in the Rainy River House and almost get arrested all because he didn't like the fact that Wayne was coming on to Maude. Anyway, my folks insisted Larry stay the night, which was fine with him. Mom and Dad were all excited about the coming engagement, the four of us devouring warmed-over spaghetti, and Mom and Dad seeming so *satisfied* with themselves. But I couldn't get out of my mind that I had never seen Larry fly off the handle the way he did because of Maude, and maybe he liked Maude more than he should. Then I simply told myself I was absolutely screwy to be jealous of Maude.

Fourteen

Maude

Running barefoot with Linda, the air cool, the moonlight ghostly on the sand traps and mounds and sweeps of grass on the deserted golf course, I threw myself against the wind recklessly, trying to get free of my feelings about Larry.

Moonshadows of the tall pine trees lay stretched across the grass. Breathless, I flung myself facedown. The cut blades of grass prickled my mouth. Lately it seemed my mind was manufacturing endless questions. Who was that girl I saw in the mirror when I did my makeup each morning? What did I want from Dolph? And Wayne, wasn't being with him too much like playing with fire? Why did I feel so at ease with Dolph and he with me, and what was the spark missing between us? And Larry — I had a thousand questions I wanted to ask Larry but never would. Larry, who kept slipping into my thoughts everywhere.

And then I heard his voice, Larry's voice,

from faraway, calling my name. I sat bolt upright on the grass and swept my eyes across the moon-drenched golf course.

"Maude! Maude!"

It *was* Larry's voice. I saw a distant figure in the moonlight, out near the fifteenth hole, not far from the darkened clubhouse.

"Larry?" I answered his call. "Over here!"

"Hey!" He came toward me, through patches of shadow and moonlight, his hair pale silver in the cold light as if snow had fallen on his head.

"Hello," Larry said, close enough now for me to see the crooked half-smile on his face.

I was standing motionless, yet my face, my hands, my arms, seemed to be flowing toward him.

"Are you laughing at me?" I asked.

"No."

"You think my running is ridiculous?"

"No, Maude. No way. The opposite of ridiculous."

"Oh," I said.

"Doesn't it seem peculiar to you, Maude, that I just happened to be here on this golf course in the middle of the night?"

His eyes had a boyish twinkle that reached into my heart and made me shiver and want to run away.

"At the picnic you said you run at night with Linda on the golf course. It stuck in my mind. Flaky girl with dog skimming over exclusive grass. I got curious, like I had to see for myself. Been parked near your house for hours. Finally saw you sneak out and start running. The two of you look like . . . I don't know . . . just very free. And then I felt bad for spying on you, so I called out."

"Thanks, Larry."

"For spying on you?"

"You weren't spying. You were watching."

Our eyes met and then Larry ducked his head away uncomfortably. "Is that how you feel when you're running, Maude? Free?"

"I don't know. When Linda and I run this way, I almost feel I don't exist anymore. I'm sorry. I know I sound dumb."

"No, hey, I like the way you sound." That uncomfortable look again in his eyes. "It's very hard to lie to you, Maude."

"I don't believe you lie to me."

"I lie to everyone, but they don't know it."

"What lies do you tell, Larry?"

He turned his back and walked a few steps away. The moonlight vanished for a moment behind a cloud. Larry walked back to me. "Maude, I don't tell lies, but I don't tell the truth."

"I don't understand, Larry."

"Want to hear something funny?" He whipped his head up and laughed harshly. "When I was fourteen, when I was fourteen years old, I was so twisted up inside, so miserable, I knew I had to get help. So I started a bank account so I could save money and go and pay somebody to help me. Of course, I had this great front. Larry the athlete, Larry the top student, Larry the social success. But I felt so bad. No matter how many friends I had, I walked around with a hole in me and nothing could fill it. I worked after school, weekends, summers, to save money so I could pay a psychologist to talk to me. I've been seeing her twice a week for the past year. Nobody knows, not Jen, not my father."

"You could tell Jen, Larry."

"No!" His eyes flared at me.

"Jen respects you. It would help her to know."

"No!" He grabbed my shoulders, his powerful fingers hurting me. "And I don't want anybody else to know! Nobody!"

Then his hands fell away from me, his voice gentle again. "I didn't mean to shout. I thought I'd feel great once I told somebody."

"Don't you?" I said weakly.

Larry took my hand. "I'm glad I told you, Maude. I knew you must have suffered a lot growing up, so I knew you'd understand."

"I do, Larry. I do."

We walked together to his truck. He waved and drove off. I stood rooted to the spot, long after the truck had disappeared. Why had he really come to watch me run? Was it a spur-of-the-moment decision to tell me things no one, not even Jen, knew about him? Jen's face rose up in my mind. No one since Nancy had been so good to me. Larry loved Jen. He would tell her too, about himself. But for the moment I was the only one who knew and I felt so close to him. I could see how people get addicted to things. I was getting addicted to thinking about Larry.

Fifteen

Jen

Jealousy! One little drop gets in your blood and BLAT! the paranoia takes over. Yes, I was jealous of Maude. It was horribly unfair to her, sure, but I couldn't help it. I began to feel more and more like she was this rich inner person and I was this beautiful empty shell of a person. I reminded myself a thousand times that Larry had chosen *me* to get engaged to, not Maude, so really my jealousy was groundless, but you can't imagine how often nasty thoughts kept sprouting in me.

I guess I figured if I was so sick and tired of myself, Larry would have to be sick and tired of me too, but he didn't realize it yet. After two years of going steady with me, maybe Maude would be a welcome change for him. Sounds dumb, but that's where my head was.

And speaking of my head, that week I went out and blew thirty dollars, almost the last thirty dollars in my hard-earned savings account, to buy a wig, a coal black wig, and don't ask me why I suddenly *had* to buy that particular black wig.

As for the Love Experiment, frankly it was beginning to get on my nerves and I was ready to dump it, except that my other feelings for Maude, real caring feelings, wouldn't let me drop her when she was riding high and would probably do a real Humpty Dumpty without the Love Experiment to keep her from falling off the wall.

Three, four times a day I saw Larry, in the lunchroom, in class, at football practice, at home, wherever; and he kissed me and I kissed him and he didn't have the faintest idea that my feelings were the pits.

"Your mother wants us to make a list of people we want to invite to our engagement party."

"Larry, I don't *want* to make a list. I don't even want an engagement party. No one has engagement parties anymore. I'm only doing it for my mother."

"Well, she's got to know how many people are coming."

"And I don't want to invite *people*. A few friends, fine. But not *people*. People makes it sound like we're planning to rent out Yankee Stadium."

"I've got to invite Dolph and Wayne and Coach Bergman and my father, and that means Coach Bergman's wife, plus my father's going to insist I invite Uncle Willy, and I can't invite Dolph without at least inviting Al Medina and Charlie Cooper and Richie Flanagan from the team. Of course, you're inviting Maude and your mob of girl friends, plus — "

Larry went on with our list, and I nodded in the right places, but I hardly heard a word. He's talking lists and I'm feeling feelings, and never the twain shall meet. Talking about feelings to a man is like talking about icebergs to some dude in the Gobi Desert. Most men wouldn't know a feeling if it punctured their eardrums!

It occurred to me that maybe I should reveal my true loony tunes to Maude — how stupidly jealous I was because I had sort of created her and she was sort of outdoing me, and how I was afraid Larry didn't know how much better he liked Maude than he liked me, and how on top of *that* I wasn't even sure I wanted to be engaged to Larry or anybody, and what was I going to do with my life to make it mean something.

I had the house to myself. Who wanted it? I lay in bed alone and swore that if I ever had kids I would never be so proud the way my parents were of me — even from age ten and eleven — that I could stay all by myself, and make myself dinner, and put myself to bed without seeming unhappy or complaining about it. Even at eighteen you can sometimes feel like about three years old and want your mommy and daddy to give you a kiss goodnight.

Just as I was drifting off to sleep it began

to dawn on me that maybe all of us involved in the Love Experiment to transform Maude were going to be put through our own pretty heavy changes too, as if some mysterious force was determined to teach us not to play around lightly with another person's life.

Sixteen

Maude

I ran with Linda every night, and every night I listened and hoped and imagined Larry calling me and moving toward me again across the grass of the golf course.

Before Jen swept me into her life I had wanted very little. But now I wanted so much. I wanted friends. I wanted admiration. I wanted people to be proud of me. And I wanted Larry. I was greedy to make up for all the years of being nobody.

I was falling in love with Larry. At the same time Wayne attracted me so much, in a disturbing way that scared me. I didn't like being churned up by Wayne. I also didn't want to be scared; too much like the old Maude. There was no hope for me with Larry so why not see what happens with Wayne, take some risks, have a sense of adventure?

Wayne kept asking for dates and I kept giving him excuses. I did see Dolph a lot; he asked me out regularly, but he didn't seem as interested in me as before. We had good times but Dolph often had a glum expression and his thoughts wandered from what we were talking about. Then in school I saw him talking to Mary Jane Jackson, warm and animated like the old Dolph. He took me aside and told me he was planning to go steady with Mary Jane. I was genuinely glad for him. Lots of boys were asking me for dates, although I turned them down. Dolph did tell me all his problems with Mary Jane, how she made him miserable but he loved it, how he had taken her out to Harvey's ranch and she didn't like the horses, and she didn't like the food, and she didn't really like Harvey and Laura, and she sneezed most of the time because of her allergies. I enjoyed my new role with Dolph.

Wayne was exciting and Dolph was comfortable, but Larry was the one I thought about constantly. And he was the one I could never have a relationship with.

Meanwhile, at home, trouble had been brewing for weeks. The house messy. Dishes greasy in the sink. Dirty laundry. No food in the fridge. Often the boys had to get their own breakfast or dinner. It takes a lot of extra hours for a girl to be glamorous and have a social life. Often Dad found nothing on the stove for him to heat up when he came home. He must have resented it but he said nothing. We had lost the habit of talking things over like father and daughter. Then a letter came home from school about Mark and Stevie: failing to do their homework, failing to bring bag lunches to school, dirty hair, dirty ears, torn clothes. . . .

"And another thing!" Dad shouted at me all the complaints he'd been storing up since I'd started taking an interest in my own life. I don't believe I'd ever heard him shout at me. Accidentally, I knocked a glass off the table and it shattered.

"Pick that up, Maude! Every piece of it!"

My shoulders began to shrink together and I bent down over the shattered glass. Then I caught myself. "No! No! Hire yourself a housekeeper! I'm sorry about the boys but I'm glad I've changed! I like myself this way! Ever since Nancy died I've felt guilty because I knew it was she, not you, who wanted to adopt me. So I worked hard to deserve to be here. Well, I *do* deserve to be here! And if you don't want me the way I am, say so!"

I ran out of the house in tears, my father calling, "Maude! Stop!"

When I came back hours later, Dad was hunched over coffee in the kitchen. He looked worn, older.

"I'm sorry, Dad."

Staring into his cup, he stirred the coffee slowly. "I've been . . . selfish, Maude. I'm going to hire a housekeeper."

Victory for me, but I hated it, because he looked so defeated. I needed him to say something special. About me being his daughter. About the changes I'd made. But he just sipped his coffee and stared out the window.

A few minutes later, in my room, I heard Dad's car start up and drive off. It was after midnight. My makeup was off and I massaged a night cream over my face. Something clattered against my window. Again, pebbles hitting the glass panes. I opened the window. A face stared at me from way up in the branches of the pine. Wayne. He had climbed into the tree. With his guitar. He threw a pine cone at me. "Hello!" he whispered.

"Wayne, please go home!"

He sat in the pine tree with legs dangling and his guitar in his lap. "I'm writing a new song for you."

"Please don't write it in my tree," I pleaded.

He strummed his guitar and sang:

"You are afraid of what you are,
For what you are is wild,
And you were made to be a star,
Stop acting like a child.

You're scared because I dared
To show you roads you didn't know.
You think I'm just a passerby
Who'll break your heart and go."

"I knew you'd like it," he said.

"Wayne, what do you want?"

"How about a kiss for starters?"

I stared at him, exhausted from the argument with my father, and hurting, and longing. Go ahead, Maude. There's life and warmth offering itself to you. Aren't you tired of holding back? Yes! Well, then?

A sultry voice: "I'll be right down, Wayne!"

Hurriedly, I reconstructed my makeup. I

chose a filmy dress with bare shoulders. When I stepped outside in the backyard, Wayne had just ripped a huge hole in his pants, climbing down from the pine tree.

"I'm here, Wayne," I breathed.

I slid my arms around his neck and moved my face close to his. "I want you to kiss me."

He rained expert little kisses all over my face, nuzzling and kissing, then a long lingering kiss, until he saw the tears streaming out of my eyes and he croaked, "Why the hell are you *crying*?"

I shook my head and pulled away. I couldn't talk. I couldn't tell him I was crying because I wished he were Larry.

Seventeen

Jen

"Jen? Jen! Where are the names of the friends you and Larry are inviting?"

I literally had one foot out the door. I shouted back into the house, "We're inviting Linda Ronstadt, Bette Midler, Bruce Springsteen, and the Bee Gees!"

"Jen, I am not in the mood for your sarcasm." My mother tightened her mouth like a noose around each word.

It seems that our finest moments as a family often happen when I have one foot out the door.

"Jen, this engagement party," the barrage began, "will set the tone for your whole future relationship with Larry. We want you to have the right attitude."

"Mom, the whole idea of getting engaged is pretty obsolete these days — practically a fossil! But as long as we're having a party, all I want is a few friends, whole wheat pretzels, and yogurt, not a Broadway musical."

"That's not what Larry wants, my dear!"

"Sometimes I think Larry is getting engaged to you two, not me."

"We've been married a long time, Jen. We only want to use our experience to help you."

"I don't want a marriage like yours."

My mother's face looked like wax about to melt.

"I'm sorry, Mom, but it's like you've been battering at me lately. All I mean is, I want my own style of relationship. I don't want to copy someone else's."

"*Battering* you?" For a moment I thought my mother was going to cry and I knew I would cry too and how beautiful it would be for us to cry together, but suddenly her face shut tight and she slammed the front door between us.

I was angry; anger like it had been stored up a thousand years and now came rushing over me and made me want to shout and break things. Only I couldn't really be angry at my mother, because she didn't know how much she hurt me and she believed she was trying to help me. I couldn't be angry at Larry, he hadn't done anything to me, and Maude was basically an innocent guinea pig in the whole thing, so the obvious one to be angry at was myself, naturally. I wanted to be engaged to Larry, desperately, but the thought of marriage felt like I would be clamped into a pattern, the pattern my parents lived in, the pattern they were squeezing me into with Larry. I wanted Larry but I hated the pattern.

Somehow I connected all these feelings to Maude. She had lived outside the usual pattern, until I had helped her become glamorous, and then everybody discovered she was so *genuine*, which made *me* seem to myself more and more shallow. And jealous.

I felt so trapped. Afraid to be real and not even knowing what the real of me was. Afraid to risk losing Larry. Afraid to hurt Maude if I dropped the Love Experiment. Afraid to turn my parents against me. And furious at myself for being afraid.

That's when I did a dumb thing. I looked up Goldhammer in the Southhope telephone directory. After calling three unrelated Goldhammers, I heard Sonny's voice.

"Sonny, this is Jen Robbins, alias Ingrid Measles."

"Stay where you are, I'll be right over!"

The place where Sonny drove me was a sort of a farm halfway between Southhope and Lakeside, two big ramshackle wooden houses, a big barn, a smaller barn converted into an auto repair shop, and a whole army of people living there, everybody some kind of relative of Sonny's — grandparents, brothers, sisters, a retired fireman who was Sonny's "Pa" and a lady who was Sonny's "Ma." Sonny proudly introduced me to everybody as "Ingrid Measles," which made me an instant success. It was just an ordinary run-of-the-mill supper to them, but to me it was how I had daydreamed a real family could be. Cooking and gossiping and arguments and laughing and bear hugs and eating together and washing dishes. I found myself being quieter, no jokes, no smart remarks, just at ease with people and comfortable. When Sonny drove me home I thanked him because I had been able to forget all my so-called troubles.

"When will I see you?"

"I don't know, Sonny."

"That's the wrong answer, Ingrid." His voice hardened.

"Sonny, I like you, but I'm still getting engaged."

His face clouded. "I'm not some high school punk you play games with, Jen."

The bottom fell out of my stomach, but I said, very cool, "I know. Please don't drive so fast, Sonny."

He slowed to a normal speed. The menace drained out of his face. He told me impossible stories about the characters in his family. At my house I said I liked his family, and he said any time I wanted to come again just give him a call. He stared at me as if he were reading my thoughts and then his car roared away.

It occurred to me then that Sonny and Maude had a powerful thing in common — they made me completely unafraid of looking bad. When I was with either of them I didn't have to be so smart and with it and funny. They gave me a taste of how free it might feel if I could ever dare drop all my phony success games.

Some days later a certain girl friend of mine informed me that someone had seen Larry in his pickup truck at six in the morning getting gas and heading out of town with a girl beside him and that the girl he had with him was none other than Maude Harris.

Eighteen

Maude

I lay on my bed fully dressed, watching the last stars disappear and the first sunlight touch the pine tree. The streets were silent. Then a truck stopped and someone whistled. I tiptoed downstairs.

His face was tense, tired. He said hello. I said hello. We stopped for gas, then the pickup truck rolled into high gear out of town and I let myself sink into the motion of the road.

Eight hours of driving lay ahead, four hours there, four back. Eight hours alone with him. Larry had chosen to tell me things about himself, about his psychologist and about his mother, things no one else knew. I stared at the small white scar on his forehead and wondered. His hands moved strongly and smoothly on the steering wheel.

"Could we talk?" he said. "I'm nervous. I always like to jabber when I'm nervous."

"I'm not good at jabbering, Larry. Wish I was."

"You'll learn. Ask me a question, anything."

"Are you . . . are you glad we're going?"

His face tightened. "You talked me into it."

"All I did was say I'd go with you. You *should* take Jen."

"My therapist agrees with you."

"Then call Jen now, ask her, Larry."

"I don't do everything my therapist says."

"Why not?" I asked naively.

Larry smiled a brief crooked smile, shouting over the clamor of a passing trailer truck: "Because I'm dumb!"

We paid a toll and crossed a bridge. We came through a tunnel and headed toward hills. Larry said, "I will tell Jen. In my head I know she'll understand but in my guts I don't trust anyone."

"You're trusting me," I said in a small voice.

He shifted gears. The road angled higher. The sun appeared and disappeared as the road wound upward through folds of hills. I talked about Mark and Stevie and Dad and Nancy and math and Linda, more talk than I'd talked in my lifetime, because Larry needed me to.

"You lied," he said. "You're very good at jabbering." The one subject I didn't jabber about was Jen. There had been a change in the way she related to me, a distance that I hesitated to talk about with Larry. Jen continued to call me, seek me out, include me, bubbling away with ideas for my new image, but she didn't appear as natural and spontaneous. A stiffness, a remoteness, showed through her. Was she able to sense how much

I cared about Larry? She couldn't possibly be jealous. Not Jen.

I wished we could say the truth to each other. I didn't want to love Larry. It had just happened. Maybe I was only imagining the touch of coldness in Jen's eyes.

A pothole in the road jolted Larry's pickup and brought me back from troubled thoughts of Jen to the reality of Larry and me alone in the truck. I wondered how Dad would react to the note I had left, which merely explained that I was off with a friend and would be back around dinnertime. So far Dad had given me a pretty free rein in my new social life. What would happen if he decided to interfere? I imagined myself giving in to him and going back to the way things had been. The thought of it twisted my stomach into knots.

"Hey, I could use some more jabbering, please?" Larry said, half-joking, half-pleading.

I jabbered for him.

Larry's forehead knotted up when we saw the square, mottled-gray building, rows of barred windows, behind it several smaller older brick buildings and cottages and a wide blacktopped parking lot, all surrounded by a high spiked fence. Oak Valley State Hospital.

Larry parked the pickup, turned off the engine, sat there stiff in the driver's seat, both arms flat on the steering wheel. "Don't know if I can handle it, Maude."

"Do you want to go back, Larry?"

"No."

He stared through the windshield. Heat waves were rising from the black asphalt, making the hills in front of us quiver and shimmer. "No," he repeated.

I thought how little I knew about people, about myself. Here was Larry who could stand calmly poised to fling a pass while three or four linemen charged at him on the football field, yet he was sweating with fear at the idea of seeing his mother again. Only days ago, it seemed, Larry had suddenly, awkwardly, spilled out the truth about his mother being in a mental hospital. No one knew but me. The last time he had seen her, ten years ago, she had screamed at him, terrified him. The memory gave him nightmares. He lived with the fear that someday he might become like her. His therapist had suggested he see her again, now that he was no longer a child, and rid himself of the fear, but Larry had refused. His father never visited her either; his father worked the night shift as a guard five nights, drove a bus part-time weekends, came home, ate in front of the TV set, went to sleep. I had said to Larry, "If it was *my* mother, you'd make me go."

That was when he asked me to go with him.

She was slumped in a wheelchair when we saw her, outdoors behind the hospital. Other patients were playing cards, walking, reading, staring, their faces bored, depressed, suspicious. Many seemed drugged. Larry's mother had a young thin face, gray vacant eyes, and her hair badly needed combing.

A distance away, the nurse said dryly, "Refuses to walk. Nothing wrong with her." Then, as we came near: "Helen, this is your son Larry and a friend of his, to visit you."

His mother kept staring in the other direction. Larry glanced at the nurse, who motioned us to sit down on a bench facing the wheelchair.

"Excuse me," the nurse said briskly and left us.

His mother turned her head slowly, her face masklike, indifferent, and stared high over our heads at a cloud.

Larry said haltingly, "How . . . How are you . . . mother?"

Still staring at the cloud, she started to chuckle, then let her head slump forward and her hands hang limp.

I reached out to lift her up, but Larry stopped me. "Don't," he said. The shadow of a cloud moved across the ill-kept grass. The nurse returned.

Once again the pickup truck took us past miles of fruit trees. Behind the clouds the rays of the sun broke into long streams of light.

"Will you see her again?" I asked, quietly.

"No," he said. "Maybe. I don't know. Maybe I will."

I nodded.

He stopped the truck off the road and looked at me, his face very young, pale, uncertain. He brushed his sandy, soft hair away from his forehead. Suddenly we were holding each other, his mouth touching my cheek, my mouth. We kissed each other and held tight.

"I love you, Larry," I murmured without thinking.

He pulled away. "I shouldn't have kissed you. I'm sorry. Jen . . ."

A chill went through me.

"I have to take Jen . . . *there* . . . so she knows."

He swerved the pickup truck back onto the road. I can't describe what my emotions were.

It had rained in Lakeside while we were gone, the leaves on the trees glistening and dripping. I kissed Larry on the mouth one last time in my life and ran from the pickup truck into the house.

Nineteen

Jen

When Carol Gomez told me that Larry and Maude had been seen together at six o'clock in the morning in his pickup truck driving away from town, I pretended to know all about it. "He was driving Maude because *I* asked him to," I said sweetly, and before Carol could box me into a corner by asking me where they were going so early, I pinched her cheek cheerfully and added, "How did *you* see them anyway, you haven't opened your sleepy little eyes that early since you were a baby."

As soon as I could split from Carol and have a few minutes alone to think, I felt as if someone had flattened me with a steamroller. Larry and Maude behind my back — they didn't even respect me enough to tell me to my face. All my suspicions about Larry having eyes for Maude were confirmed. And all my rotten feelings about myself came pouring in as if a dam had broken.

I went to my next two classes in a daze but forced myself to keep up the Jen Robbins image, lighthearted, no care in the world, especially when two other so-called friends told me the same story as Carol Gomez.

The question was, how should I go about confronting Larry and Maude? Face them together or talk to them one at a time? I didn't have to decide, because Larry caught up to me in the hallway, his face very serious: "Let's get out of here, Jen, I've got to talk to you."

Getting into the old blue pickup truck and sitting beside Larry where *she* had sat, I longed to shock him with some horrible act, such as spitting at the windshield. Did I have bitter, poisonous words for him! By the time we drove to the beach and walked across the sand to an isolated place we knew between two big dunes, we had spoken about four syllables of conversation, including "Beach?" and "Okay" and "Good."

We kicked off our shoes, leaned against the dunes, watched the sea oats take a beating from the wind. Larry stared moodily toward the horizon. I stared moodily at Larry.

"Well, this sure has been a marvelous and unforgettable ten minutes," I said. "You have any water or soda in the truck, while I'm waiting for you to talk to me?"

"No," he muttered, fishing something from his pocket. "Want some chewing gum?"

"No, thanks, Larry, I can't drink chewing gum."

"It's very informative, talking to you, Jen. I feel I'm learning everything there is to know about dumb jokes."

"Please, sit there a moment longer without moving — I want to forget you just the way you are."

He grinned, pulled me close to him, held me tight, his cheek against my ear, his skin warm from the sun. I kept my arms around him, wishing we could stay that way always and never have to mention why he'd been with Maude at six in the morning.

"Jen, there are things you don't know about me." The warmth was out of his voice. "Things I have to tell you."

I stiffened, attacking. "Maybe I can save you time. Is Maude involved?"

Surprised, he squinted at me. "Yes and no," he said, scooping a handful of sand and spreading his fingers and watching the sand stream down. "If it wasn't for Maude I probably would go ahead and get engaged and never tell you."

I stood there with my hands on my hips, challenging him. "I suppose I better run back to town and find her and thank her on my hands and knees for all she's done for me!"

"Jen, Maude was trying to help me."

"Sure, sure, dear darling Saint Maude! She's been giving you those humble adoring puppy-dog looks since the first day we started this idiot experiment. And you fell for it!"

"No! It's just that I could talk to her about

144

certain things I couldn't say to anyone else, because she's not like us, she doesn't judge people."

I was boiling. "I suppose you drove her out of town at six in the morning so the two of you could go walking barefoot in some meadow and not judge each other!"

"I can't talk about it when you sound like that."

"You can't talk about it but the rest of the school sure can jiggle their jaws, having a good laugh on *me*! Tell me you didn't even kiss her!"

He turned his jaw toward the waves, and I knew he couldn't deny kissing her.

"Pardon me, but I'm bailing out of this airplane before it crashes." I jumped up and headed quickly toward the edge of the sea, my hands in my pockets, letting the wind whip through my hair. I heard Larry yell, "Jen, wait!"

I started running where the waves had formed loops of foam on the sand and again I heard Larry calling "Jen!" and a whole bunch of seashells cut into my feet, but I kept running over them, crushing them, and a sudden rush of the sea soaked my pants, and a gust of wind whipped spray into my face, but I kept running. Then Larry grabbed me from behind and I tried to tear myself away but he gripped my wrists between us.

"You're acting like an idiot over nothing!" he shouted.

"Get your hands off me!" I yelled back. "I don't want to be engaged to you! Not ever!"

He dropped my wrists. "You're making a mistake, Jen."

"I hope I make lots of mistakes from now on! It's about time! I'm going to make mistakes all over the place!"

I yelled at him through the sound of the waves and I felt as if I were smashing into pieces all the years of my being nice Jen, beautiful Jen, smart Jen, breaking the old Jen like those seashells underfoot.

Then Larry threw the keys to the pickup truck at my feet and yelled, "You take the truck, I'll get home myself!" and he broke into a run, the wind puffing out the back of his jacket and wet sand flying from his heels.

Twenty

Maude

The phone rang. My first thought was Larry. I was greedy for even a word with him. Foolish. I hadn't seen him or Jen at lunch and I was worried because Mindy had asked me, between bites of her tuna fish, whether Larry and I had a nice time in his truck the other morning.

The voice on the phone said his name was Eric, Mary Jane had introduced us last week, would I go out with him after the Medford game. "No" was on the tip of my tongue. I didn't want to be with anyone who wasn't Larry. Yet I knew I should date other boys, put space between Larry and me. Then I heard the sound of Larry's pickup truck. "I can't, Eric," I blurted, "but call me next week!"

Some sounds you never forget. Larry's truck had its own special bouncy rattle, a deep cough in the engine, squeaky brakes, a rumble in the muffler. "Larry!" I called.

The door opened on the driver's side. Jen's face emerged, staring up at me as if I were someone she had never seen before. I felt a terrible tightening in my stomach. Jen raced up the front steps and leaned on the buzzer. One of my brothers must have let her in. Footsteps pounded up the staircase. Jen tore open the door to my room and threw it shut behind her.

"The experiment is over, Maude, as of now."

"What experiment?"

"The Love Experiment."

"I don't understand, Jen."

"The Great Lakeside High Love Experiment, Maude. Remember when we met by accident, when I came to your door to sell beauty stuff and we recognized each other from school?"

"I spilled the apple cider on your shoes."

"Well, it wasn't an accident, Maude!"

"Yes, it was. I spilled — "

"My coming to your door wasn't an accident! It was all arranged. I planned it. I wanted to meet you."

Jen's face was hard to look at, there was so much anger in it. "It was part of the Love Experiment," she went on. "Like when I had the bike accident on your lawn. You were incredibly gullible. It was no accident. It was a fake. A way to force me and Larry and Wayne and Dolph into your life."

"Why?" My voice sounded so weak.

"Dolph and Wayne started that phony competition for dates with you. Larry and I dragged you with us everywhere. That was the Love Experiment, to see if we could take a nobody and make her somebody, pretending she was really desirable."

As Jen spoke, my body seemed to be caving in on me.

"You were just a guinea pig. It was my idea, an experiment, to do something the four of us would remember, really jazz up our senior year."

"Larry, Wayne, Dolph — all of you — *pretending* to like me?"

"And it worked, Maude. You're a big success!"

"Please. I don't want to hear any more. Please."

"Don't knock it, Maude. We worked hard giving you a free ride. We swore we'd never tell you or anyone that it was an experiment. Even when I suspected that Larry had eyes for you — I *still* would've tried to go on helping you. But now the whole school knows you went sneaking off with Larry in his truck!"

Jen's voice was choked with tears, anger, hurt. I reached toward her but she pulled away. "Jen, didn't Larry tell you where we were going in his truck?"

"He admitted he kissed you!" Her voice lashed at me. "Is he lying, Maude? He kissed you and you liked it a lot, didn't you, Maude?"

I couldn't answer.

"Well, we're not getting engaged, thanks to you!" She threw some keys on the floor. "*You* give him back his keys!"

Numb, I stood there staring at the empty

space in the doorway. Heard her running down the steps. Heard the front door slam.

The keys to Larry's truck lay on the floor where Jen had thrown them. I bent down to pick up the keys. Tears dropped from my face. I sank to my knees on the rug. What Jen had told me was like powerful, terrible fingers ripping my insides apart. With Larry's keys clutched in my fist, I held my arms around my stomach and rocked back and forth hopelessly. All the friendship, all the caring, all the good times, nothing but an experiment. Jen, Larry, Dolph, Wayne — now it made sense why suddenly they had chased after me, including me; it had seemed so casual, all their smiles and friendly talks. An experiment. It sounded so inhuman. I found myself moaning softly mournful sounds from deep in my throat. I wanted to die. I was nothing but a guinea pig to them.

I washed my face, scrubbed off all the makeup, rubbed my skin fiercely with a dry towel, as if I could clean away the falseness. I stared around my room. The feelings of betrayal and horrible embarrassment seemed to be spreading outward. I ran from the house. Space. I needed space.

In a daze I walked and walked, looking down at the sidewalk whenever I passed anyone. I must have walked for hours, going over and over the same awful thoughts. How innocent and trusting I had been, not to suspect from the beginning that the four most popular kids in school don't suddenly adopt

Maude Harris as their mascot. I had reached Miller's Hill, driven by a need to go and go and go until I dropped from exhaustion. The climb to the top of the hill happened in a blur of tears.

I'll go back to the way I was, I thought, back to the old Maude, the old life, the Maude who *was* — before Jen began her Love Experiment.

At home, I flung myself through the front door. Without any plan, I attacked the loads of unwashed clothes, dirty dishes, floors to be cleaned, all the results of my involvement with Jen and my big new life. Well, that new life was over! I threw myself into the housework as if it could somehow erase Jen and all the things that had happened in the Love Experiment.

Everything went wrong. The washing machine overflowed, I slipped on floor wax and nearly broke my spine. It was like my old self suddenly speeded up and distorted.

It was no use trying to go back to the way I used to be. I couldn't and I didn't want to.

I ran up to my room. From the window I could see Mark and Stevie playing football across the street with a neighbor's son. I grabbed a large green suitcase from the bottom of my closet. Jerkily snatching at objects, I scooped them into my suitcase. I wrote a note: "Dear Dad, Stevie, Mark, I need to be alone awhile. I promise to be careful and take care of myself. Don't worry. My typing is good, also my steno, I'll get a job. Will call you when I'm settled. Sincerely, Maude. P.S., Please love Linda."

With a piece of Scotch tape I stuck the note on my mirror. I saw the hair, long black hair, loose, my hair. I gripped the back of my hair in my fist and pulled tight until the roots hurt. The scissor fitted into my hand. Moments later the waste basket was black with hair. It didn't make me feel better.

The phone rang. I didn't want to answer. I picked up the receiver.

"Hello? Maude?" The high, glassy voice of Carol Gomez tinkled at me. "Anyone there? Hello? Hello?"

I hung up. Was Carol part of the experiment too? How many people knew I was a guinea pig? A sickness of shame and loneliness swept over me.

I took one last look at my room: the cosmetics and beauty aids lined up on the dresser, in the closet all the clothes Jen had picked out for me at sales. I despised them. Or did I? Who was I going to be: the old Maude, the new Maude, or somebody in between?

I rammed the sexy clothes and the cosmetics into the green suitcase and called a cab. On the way to the bus station I sank into the leather seat of the taxi and hid my face from the street and prayed not to see anyone who knew me.

The bus station was empty. A fat man in the ticket booth scratched his nose when I asked, "When is the next bus?"

"Where to?" he yawned.

"Oh. Uh." Larry had been offered a football scholarship to a school in Colorado. "Denver," I said.

The man reached for his schedule.

"That's in Colorado," I said.

"Thanks," he said sarcastically. "Bus arrives in two hours."

I was suddenly afraid to wait two hours. "Anything sooner?"

"Going where, Miss?"

"Uh . . ." Larry had also been offered a scholarship to a school in Texas. "Houston?"

"Okay. Half an hour. One-way or round-trip?"

All the seats in the rows of molded plastic chairs were empty. I sat with a magazine. I was so jumpy I read the same paragraph four times. I tried to do a crossword puzzle. Glancing up, I saw someone on a seat at the opposite side of the station. It was Larry, leaning forward, his hands together between his knees. I stared feverishly at my crossword puzzle but it blurred because my eyes were suddenly wet. Then I saw someone lower himself into a seat at the far end of my row. Wayne. He didn't look at me. He crossed his knees. Then I saw Dolph sit down five or six seats away from Larry and begin cleaning his fingernails. A metallic voice boomed: "Express bus to Houston arriving at Gate Three."

Knees wobbling, I picked up my suitcase and walked. Larry stood up, Dolph stood up, Wayne stood up. They followed me to Gate Three. People were filing off the bus.

"Maude," Larry said. "Mark saw your note and called me. I called Jen. She said how you know about the experiment."

I stepped into the bus, gave my ticket to the driver. Dolph, Larry, Wayne, staring at me outside the bus as I found a seat. Larry scribbled furiously on the window with a big red magic marker: WE LOVE YOU, DUMMY!

People were staring at me. The bus roared away. But not very far away. I fumbled down the aisle with my suitcase. The driver, when I begged him to stop, groaned. He braked the big bus. I climbed out and the bus swept away. I saw three people running toward me, yelling. They were my friends.

Twenty-one

Jen

It was like someone injected a poison in me, my blood carried it to every cell in my body, and this whole Jekyll and Hyde thing happened. Jealous, rebellious, moody, all the things I'd never allowed myself to be. Maybe I was overreacting to the thing with Larry and Maude, but it seemed as if I'd been holding back all my true feelings for a lifetime and Larry and Maude were the actual straws that broke the camel's good-guy image.

I wanted to burst out and show everybody that I wasn't who they thought I was. Sure, I had a pang of guilt for pulling the rug out from under Maude but the moment I got home from Maude's house my guilt was forgotten because I found another neat little note from my parents about some charity bridge party they'd be at till late. I found a paper shopping bag, tore it open, wrote on it in large letters: "Dear parents, I won't be home tonight, which I know won't worry you, because you are both very very busy. Your trustworthy daughter, Jen." I laid the note on their bed.

Then I telephoned Sonny Goldhammer and asked him if he was interested in coming over. "Dynamite!" he said, very up, and then his voice for an instant had that dangerous cold-blooded sound. "What's with your engagement?"

I answered, "We pressed the self-destruct button."

While I was waiting for Sonny's white sedan to come blasting along the road from Southhope, I called Mrs. Bralver and told her I was quitting the cheerleaders. Hearing her voice fall gave me a sense of power. I could imagine her high-teased hair with a pencil in it. No, Mrs. Bralver, this isn't a joke. Yes, Mrs. Bralver, something *did* happen. No, Mrs. Bralver, I can't talk about it. Yes, Mrs. Bralver, I'm sure I'll feel sorry. Yes, Mrs. Bralver, I believe you *are* concerned about me.

I put myself into the hottest shower I could stand, steam billowing around the bathroom. I slipped into a skirt with a slit that should have been illegal and a loose-fitting blouse. I covered my head with the black wig I had never had the guts to wear before and did my eyes and face in a very icy way with eye shadow glittering like aluminum foil. I wore my most expensive fake fingernails which I painted black, probably because Larry hated black makeup.

But Sonny flipped, couldn't keep his eyes off me, and when I suggested we drive to

Lake Murdoch to see the sunrise over the lake, he said that sounded pretty flaky. I said I thought he liked flaky girls. He said it depended on how flaky, because it's a seven-hour drive each way, and since when do your folks let you out overnight? I said we'd get back tomorrow just in time to see Medford destroy Lakeside. He said he thought I was a big Lakeside fan, and what's so hot about watching the sunrise over Lake Murdoch anyway? I said we could make a bet: he drives there, I drive back, whoever makes better time wins the bet. He asked what he would win. I told him that if he won I would wash his car once a week for a month but if I won he'd have to take me out to dinner once a week for a month.

Sonny cracked a grin so wide you could practically see the bones stand at attention and said, "You've got yourself a bet!"

I shook Sonny's hand: "Good luck, Cannonball!"

He said, "*Cannonball*? Hey, I like it. Fits me. Cannonball Goldhammer."

I never saw driving like the driving Sonny did all the way to Lake Murdoch. He was better than good. We had bought a half dozen Big Macs and a six-pack of soda and lots of chocolate-covered raisins, and the drive was a blur of headlights and flashing red taillights. Once when the talk petered out between us I was on the verge of making a lot of bright chitchat but I thought of Maude and she reminded me that I never again had to fill up the silence with conversational turkey stuffing. In the dark of the car, lighted only by the dashboard dials and the flash of passing headlights, the silence between Sonny and me became good. Then east of us, slowly, the darkness dissolved and the stars began to look watery.

Sunrise happened over Lake Murdoch at exactly two minutes and ten seconds after six o'clock in the morning. We sat cross-legged on the top of Sonny's car and sloshed down coffee and got ourselves sticky with the sugar from doughnuts and laughed at the dumbest things we said to each other, and Sonny kissed me easy on the mouth and asked if I was ready to wash his car, because there was no way I could make better time than six hours fifty-eight minutes.

"Watch me!" I said.

"Drive!" he said.

I drove. I drove my eyelids off. Sonny didn't say much and I didn't either, because I was driving at least as fast as he did but I wasn't controlling the car so much as the car was controlling me and I should have slowed down but I felt a hard knot of stubbornness in me. Sonny acted very cool, though I noticed him hooking on his safety belt. I had this feeling that I was losing something, something so important; yet I didn't know what it was and I couldn't think very clearly. I hated the feeling of having to start my whole life again with someone I hardly knew, like Sonny Goldhammer, and my foot pinned the accelerator to the floor and Sonny shouted at the top of his lungs, "Watch out!"

Twenty-two

Maude

Mark and Stevie burst into the room and threw themselves on the bed with me, shouting, "Wake up! Larry and Dolph and Wayne are in the kitchen!" Linda barking, the boys tumbling me out of bed, I couldn't help laughing.

Some days you like your face, some days you wish it would get lost. The mirror reflected a nice face, my face. Even without makeup, I liked myself. Even with my hair sliced off.

Then came Jen-thoughts and my mood took a nose dive. It was the first time in my life I ever hated anybody.

Larry will tell Jen the truth about why I was with him, the truth about his mother, his therapy. Jen will understand and everything will be okay. For them. But nothing will ever be the same for me.

Twice during the night I had woken up to images of Jen staring cruelly at me from the darkness of my own mind. I had imagined her voice: "Guinea pig! Guinea pig!"

159

Coming slowly down the stairs, I heard Dolph and Larry laughing in the kitchen. And Wayne tickling his guitar. Motionless, I listened. My dad and brothers sounded happy. They didn't know the whole thing had been an experiment.

Yet I realized I shouldn't cling to the hurt. Larry and Wayne and Dolph had come after me at the bus station. They had said in the beginning it was just an experiment, but not anymore. You, they said, are part of us, whatever way it happened. And I had believed them.

But Jen. I couldn't forgive her. I hated her. I knew I shouldn't. I should forgive. You're supposed to be forgiving, Maude. But I didn't want to forgive Jen ever! I'd argued back and forth with myself over and over. The experiment had been Jen's idea. She had helped me more than I could say, even though it was just an experiment to her. I should be grateful for all the exciting new things in my life, no matter what she did to hurt me. But the way she'd told me had been so cruel. Yet she did have an excuse: she thought I was cheating on her with Larry. At least she hadn't retaliated by telling the whole school about the experiment. No one knew but the five of us. You should be grateful, Maude.

No! I wanted to hate her! And I realized then that some of my anger at Jen came from wanting Larry for myself.

We piled into Larry's pickup truck for the drive to the Lakeside football field. I sat with

Larry up front, alone, the others in the back of the truck. His good humor suddenly seemed to evaporate. With his jaw set tight, he dropped a bombshell. "Maude, Jen's mother called me because Jen didn't come home last night." In a low voice, almost drowned by the engine, Larry went on: "Jen's mother said she's going to call the police."

An unpleasant chill surged along the back of my neck.

At Lakeside High, Dolph and Larry hurried away to get into uniform. Wayne and I picked out seats on the fifty-yard line.

I sat there in the stands, looking at a blue bright sky, high feathery fast-moving clouds, and a small white afternoon moon. Was Jen looking at the sky? Where? Call it ESP, call it a troubled imagination, call it woman's intuition — I knew that something had happened to Jen and that she needed me.

Football cleats clacking on the wooden benches brought me back to where I was, in the deserted stands. Larry, his helmet off, was leaping from bench to bench toward me. He caught my waist in his hands. He hoisted me up in the air. "We won, Maude! We won!"

"Larry, I'm . . . I'm worried about Jen. I *know* something's happened to her!"

His expression suddenly soured, from exultation to annoyance. "Come on, Maude, we just beat Medford! Jen isn't thinking about *you*. Or me. I bet she spent the night out just to get back at us."

"I've got to find her."

"After the way she treated you?"

"Yes." I pulled away from him and dashed toward a telephone booth with Larry in pursuit.

Jen's mother told me what I needed to know: "She's been hurt. A car accident. Lakeside Hospital. Please tell Larry. I'm on my way to the hospital."

Larry, still dressed in his football uniform, shot the pickup truck out of the school parking lot and into traffic. Ahead of us, only ten or twelve blocks away, the silhouette of Lakeside General Hospital dominated the surrounding strip of markets and shops and private houses.

"Hurry, Larry, please!"

The pickup truck shuddered as it struck a pothole and swung between two slower moving sedans.

"Get out of the way, you idiot!" he shouted, and ground his teeth at a twelve-wheel trailer truck and a moving van which were blocking both sides of the street as they were signaled into parking positions by men who waved us to a stop. Half a dozen cars were backed up, stuck.

"I'll meet you there!" I said, and jumped out of Larry's pickup before he could stop me.

Out and running toward the hospital, I glanced back and saw Larry in reverse gear, one wheel up on the sidewalk, trying to work his way out of the tie-up. I turned the corner and raced the last few blocks to Lakeside General, praying for Jen, all my anger gone, the viciousness of it replaced by a flood of hope that I could somehow help her. I felt only my caring for Jen, and not emptiness.

A blue-uniformed hospital guard glared at me as I came sprinting into the lobby toward the information desk, trembling with hope for Jen to be okay.

Twenty-three

Jen

Waking up, coming from the dark bottom of somewhere pitch-black, a light far away getting brighter and closer, and then a pain stabbing my ankle and my entire body aching as if I had been punched and kicked all over, especially my face. I opened my eyes and I thought I saw my mother's face. Then I think I fell asleep and woke up again with the sun slanting through a window, and my mother still sitting there, and my jaw seemed to be clamped together. My mother took my hand and said that she loved me and that I was going to be all right, but it seemed to me that "all right" was on one side of the world and I was on the other.

My mother was incredible: patient, sensitive, answering all my questions. There were bandages over the left side of my face and right cheek. My neck was in a padded thing. Mom explained that Dad was flying to see me from a conference in San Francisco, that Sonny's car had hit a tree. He was miraculously unhurt. The car was totaled, my ankle broken, my face cut, a concussion, bad whiplash, but no one else was hurt.

"Will my face be scarred?" I asked.

That's when the doctor came in, fortunately the kind of guy who respected you even if you were still a teen-ager, and he told me without any sugar-coating that a shattered ankle heals very slowly and that the gashes on my face might cause scars. I had visions of ugly dead gray skin on my face. I wanted to creep into a corner and hide, but the doctor went on talking about my ankle, how ankles are difficult to heal, but I would be walking again.

After the doctor left, my mother told me that Sonny Goldhammer had called a dozen times to see me.

"Mom, I don't want to see anyone. Please. No one. Just you and Dad."

It doesn't entirely matter that you have conflicts with your parents or you can't *really* communicate with them about a lot of things, because sometimes, if you're lucky, they are there when you need them.

"Hi, I'm Miss Gallo." A very pretty nurse interrupted mother and me, but her smile was a definitely nonphony smile and I liked her immediately. She told me to call her Lilly and also said I had a visitor, a girl who had been waiting a long time to see me.

"No, Miss Gallo, I want to be left alone."

When Mom and Miss Gallo were gone, my spirits disintegrated.

Hours later, just before Dad arrived, Miss

Gallo told me that Larry, Wayne, and Dolph had come and gone, but the "girl" was still stubbornly waiting.

It's all upside down, I thought grimly, almost as if Maude has taken over my life and I've taken over hers. In the beginning, all Maude had wanted was to be left alone, but I kept dragging her out of hiding into the real world. Now I want to hide under a rock and *she* won't let *me* alone.

Well, I didn't care how long she sat there. I never wanted to see her or Lakeside or anyone from Lakeside ever again.

Twenty-four

Maude

Jen refused to see me, but I wouldn't leave the hospital. Stubbornly sitting there in the lobby, I had no patience to read the magazines. My eyes roamed along the immaculate walls and gleaming floor.

Elevator doors opened, closed, opened, closed. Patients, visitors, nurses, doctors, each of them different from the other, the way they tilted their heads or gestured with their hands, talking, frowning, cheerful or grim.

For a moment I wasn't Maude anymore, I was Jen, Jen in the car accident that had brought her to the hospital. I didn't know the details but I could hear the squeal of brakes, see the splintering of glass.

Something very special had happened to Jen and me because of the experiment she had set in motion. We had come close, that's the only word for it, minds and spirits almost mingling. Jen had pulled me out of a cramped little box on the shelf and forced me to be some of the wonderful things she was.

The experiment had been far more than a prank. Nobody could destroy what I had become.

It was the perfect moment for Larry to appear. "How's Jen?"

"Not good, Larry, but she's not in any danger. A nurse told me she shattered her ankle and hurt her face, a concussion, whiplash."

"Her face?" He winced. "How bad?"

"I don't know."

He sat down beside me and took my hand. I shifted uncomfortably and removed my hand.

"We caused it, Larry. You've got to tell Jen why I was in your truck that morning."

"Hey, don't make *me* the bad guy! I did what I did and Jen did what Jen did."

"But you and I should have realized how sensitive Jen is underneath."

"Maybe we don't know her as well as we think," Larry brooded, his face dark, questioning.

"But, Larry, it was our responsibility, as her friends — "

"Will you get off that responsibility kick? She acted like a thoughtless little . . . and you're defending her! First little thing didn't go her way, she threw you right down the drain!"

"That's not how I see it, Larry."

"Poor Jen had an accident and we're supposed to forgive and forget! Maybe *you* don't have normal human feelings, but I do. She's engaged to *me* and she spends the night with some bum from Southhope!"

He wheeled around and strode out of the hospital, knocking into Wayne and Dolph, who were just entering.

"What's with Larry?" Wayne asked when the two of them found me.

Dolph said, "I had to come to see Jen."

"She won't see anyone but her parents," I explained.

"We ain't just *anyone*," Dolph said.

"Sometimes when people are hurt, they want to crawl into a hole and hide," Wayne suggested.

"Not Jen," Dolph muttered, "it's not like her."

"Come on, Maude, we'll take you home," Wayne offered. "I've got my father's car."

"No, thanks. I'm staying."

"What for?"

I didn't answer.

"Man, I give up!" Wayne grunted.

Dolph stood up and pecked my cheek. "Maude, I got to mosey on home, and you're comin' with us, even if I have to get my lasso and hog-tie you."

"No."

"Don't be so ornery, dammit!"

I was ready to explode but I controlled it. "I'm *staying*!"

They left.

The hours dragged.

Jen's mother walked past, her mouth drawn tight, not saying anything, but nodding to me.

The red hand on the hospital clock took longer and longer to travel sixty seconds.

A new security guard came on duty; he looked as tired as I felt. Nobody said I had to leave. Maybe I wished they would. Darkness seemed to be seeping into the hospital lobby from the night outside the glass doors.

"It's midnight, Maude." Larry had returned.

"I know."

"You're staying here?"

"Yes."

"Does your father know?"

"I called him."

"What are you trying to prove, Maude?"

"I want Jen to know how I feel."

Larry shook his head and pulled his chin. "Look, I spoke to Jen's mother. Jen doesn't care if you or I or a whole army sit here. She doesn't *care*, Maude. She doesn't want you or me! Right this minute she probably doesn't even know you're here."

"*I* know I'm here, Larry."

"You planning to sleep sitting up or should I buy you a box of toothpicks to keep your eyes open all night?"

The sarcasm in his voice struck me like a whip.

"Okay!" He took a step toward the hospital doors, then turned. "The team is having a victory party tomorrow. I'll pick you up at your house."

"I'm sorry, Larry. I'll be here at the hospital."

He grunted loudly, "A girl with a one-way

170

mind!" He stomped past the slumping security guard and out into the dark.

Ten minutes. Twenty minutes. Twenty-five.

A hand — Larry's — dangled a bag of hamburgers and a container of milk in front of me.

"Maude," he said grandly, "may you eat of this fruit of the Big Mac tree and find friendship in your stomach forever. I know I shouldn't be joking at a time like this, Jen in the hospital hurt. I do care about her. And I care about you. The whole thing is a mess. I'm a mess." He offered me, in parting, a weak smile. This time Larry left and didn't come back. I didn't know whether to laugh or cry.

My eyelids began drooping, but I forced myself to stay awake. I longed to lift my feet up and stretch out along the plastic hospital furniture. I splashed cold water on my face in the ladies' room. As the hours passed, I became more and more stubborn. It was like a contest of wills between me and Jen. The next morning I called her room from the lobby but she hung up the moment I spoke.

I didn't spend any more nights there, but every spare hour of every day that followed I sat in the hospital lobby, sent fruitless notes, did my homework on my lap. Evenings I walked a bit on the hospital grounds, hearing the rush of wings in the darkness when I passed near a stand of pines, and looking hopefully toward the lighted window I thought might be Jen's, always believing that Jen would finally see me. Days passed and every day there was the same No.

I did succeed in having a few words with Jen's mother. She agreed to coffee in the hospital snack shop. Her mind was somewhere else. She didn't seem to hear any of my suggestions. In a flat voice she told me Jen was "fixated" against seeing anyone. She said she was sure Jen would soon "come out of it." Come out of *what*, I wondered.

I didn't stop trying to see Jen, not even after she left the hospital. Twice a day I phoned her home, always at the same times. Though Jen never picked up the phone, she *had* to know it was me calling. Jen's mother would answer and repeat, very patiently, "Sorry, Jen doesn't want to speak to anyone."

One afternoon, however, Jen's mother called *me*. She asked to meet me for lunch. She picked a plush little restaurant with many colors of glass in its Tiffany lampshades. We didn't say much until after we ordered. Then she reached across the table and took my hand and held it. Her eyes were troubled. "Thank you for not giving up, Maude."

The tips of her fingers touched her closed eyes briefly, and then she went on: "Jen *will* get well. But her ankle is slow, and she has three bad scars — at her eye, at the corner of her mouth, at her hairline."

"Mrs. Robbins, I thought plastic surgery could — "

"Do wonders, yes, but there will be definite scars."

I tried to imagine how Jen might feel about "definite scars."

"Maude, she seems so depressed. She's not my Jen anymore. Sits there, gloomy, not talking. And when *you* call and she hears me speak to you, she just stares at me."

"Should I stop calling, Mrs. Robbins?"

"No, please, don't!"

So I kept on calling. And praying.

In school my life was going a mile a minute. Jen's absence had left a vacuum in Lakeside High, and people somehow expected me to fill it. Girls came to me to gossip or talk about their problems. Boys hung around, joked, asked for dates or even advice about their steadies. Somehow the right words came out of my mouth.

As for Larry, Dolph, and Wayne, with Jen not around they seemed to need me more than ever to keep the group alive. It was as if Jen's absence had suddenly made them aware that soon we'd all probably be separated, maybe never see each other again, and they wanted to hold on to some sense of being together.

After a while we didn't discuss Jen anymore. The subject made us all ill at ease. But I never stopped thinking about her. Not even when Larry asked me out on our first conventional date.

I had feared he would ask me and planned to say no. When he surrounded me with that challenging, mystifying smile of his, flecks of gray in his blue green eyes, yes came right off my tongue.

It was all very formal. Larry rang the doorbell, shook hands with my father, told

173

him what time we'd be home, winked at Mark and Stevie, patted Linda, opened the door of his pickup truck for me to enter, and eased the truck away from my driveway until we were out of sight. We drove awhile in the twilight. Not going anywhere special. Then he said his therapist figured it was time for him to cut loose from therapy. He also said he might visit his mother again after graduation. I asked if he ever called Jen and he said he had seen Jen's mother twice but not Jen.

Then I took the plunge and asked him to tell me about the Love Experiment, how it got started, everything he remembered. His mouth formed a silent no. I said it might help me to know some details, so I wouldn't feel so much like an object they all had operated on.

Unwillingly, he began to speak about the four of them around a campfire at Cold Spring River and Jen's ideas and strategies. Listening passively, emotions churned inside me.

On the way back into town we talked about Dolph's recent decision to forget college and work toward a partnership in a small ranch with some older guy named Harvey whom Larry had never heard of. Larry couldn't understand why I seemed so pleased about Dolph's choice. He also couldn't understand why I didn't think it was terrible that Wayne had taken his father's offer of a full-time job in his belt factory. Certain things are hard to explain.

Then we saw a movie, ate popcorn, and talked to some kids from school. We talked about college, looked at the stars. Then he kissed me. A sudden kiss. A hard kiss.

"What's the matter, Maude?"

Jen was the matter, her ankle smashed, her face marred, her spirit broken.

"Larry, we shouldn't date each other."

"Why?"

"For a while."

"*Why*, Maude?"

"Jen."

"That's not fair to you and me."

"How can you switch off your feelings for her so quickly?"

"Maude, it's been happening since I first got to know *you*, only I didn't realize it."

He tried to pull me toward him, but I held back. His eyes flashed with resentment. He threw the truck into gear noisily. "Is Jen more important than us?"

"To me, yes." I ached inside as I said those words.

The pickup truck lurched away from the parking spot where we had been looking at the silhouette of the hills and the moon on the sea in the distance. Larry's voice cooled. "You're scared to let Jen go and stand on your own two feet!"

"Maybe, Larry. I don't think so."

"Jen wants us to get off her case, stay out of her life, but you keep trying to make her front-page news!"

The truck went spinning toward town.

175

Lying in bed that night with the lights off, I remembered Larry's words: *You keep trying to make her front-page news.*

That's when I got the idea. A way to reach Jen.

Twenty-five

Jen

What in the world is worse than people feeling sorry for you? Home from the hospital, I tore up all the pictures of me with Larry, and me in my cheerleader's uniform, and me with Dolph and Wayne. I looked at my face in the mirror and picked up a paperweight and let it fly. The glass shattered and when my mother and father came running to my room I was standing there out of breath, leaning on my cane to take the weight off the stiff white cast around my foot and ankle. My father stooped and picked up the pieces of broken mirror. I wished I could tell them how badly I wanted to go away and hide in the darkest corner of the universe, wherever that is.

My mother handled it better than my father. She truly didn't seem to see my scars or my cane and limp. My father tried to pretend he wasn't bothered, but his eyes showed how much it hurt him to see my face and the way I walked, and over and over he alluded to Dr. Morgan's prediction that I'd be walking unaided by midsummer and my scars would be hardly noticeable.

Mother insisted I keep up with my school-work; my teachers mailed us all the assignments, and the school informed us that I could get my diploma at graduation. Wild horses couldn't drag me into that school again, for graduation or anything else, unless they had a way of giving me my face back untouched, like it was before the accident.

A kind of shell had grown around me, an invisible shell separating me from people, but I think the shell had always been there without my really knowing it — a very pretty shell, but filled with loneliness. I was lonelier now than I had ever feared I could be, whether I sat in the backyard or in the kitchen or the basement or in my room, the loneliness never left me alone, no matter how hard Mom and Dad tried to be kind.

Was it just plain vanity that made me shun everybody? Because my face was cut up? Maybe. But it wasn't the accident alone, it was also the shame I felt about hurting Maude, and at the same time the rottenness about the way Larry and Maude had betrayed me, and — more than anything — my whole phony breezy self had collapsed.

Sure, lots of girls had much worse accidents or diseases and lots of girls lost their boyfriends or were betrayed, probably in much worse ways. Was I just exaggerating the whole affair into a tragedy? If I had any guts shouldn't I be stiff-upper-lipping it like a mature grownup? But maybe I had grown up too soon and too perfect, Jen Robbins the all-around Miss Lakeside.

Occasionally I sat at the window in my room pretending to read and fantasizing that Maude and Larry and Dolph and Wayne would come bursting into my house, rush up the stairs, throw open my door, and we would all yell and scream at each other and laugh and cry. The letters they actually sent me I never opened, just tore up. The only person, finally, who didn't stop trying to reach me was Maude.

Twice each day the phone rang like clockwork, Maude calling, I could tell from how my mother spoke to her, saying Jen didn't want to talk to anyone. Not a day passed when I didn't think that *today* she'll finally leave me alone, but Maude kept calling.

Sometimes I wanted so badly to talk to Maude. In the past it had seemed to me I was giving this poor scared empty creature big transfusions of my own wonderful self; now I began to realize that she had been maybe equally affecting me, touching lost places in me. And I began to appreciate the courage she had; not my kind of foolhardy flaunting but a real quiet little flame that burned in her.

So, a dozen times when I heard the phone ring and my mother answer and obviously it was Maude, I wanted to run and grab the phone. But the shame I felt was too great, shame that Larry had deceived me with Maude and shame that I had struck back so furiously at her.

At the same time, Mother was prodding me to consider attending graduation and I knew she meant well, but it made me sick to my stomach to imagine showing myself to all those hundreds of kids and teachers who remembered me the way I was before the accident.

And then one day a few days before graduation my mother knocked on the door of my room and handed me a package, brown wrapping, no return address. Inside was a book, the Lakeside High School Yearbook, with a bookmark sticking out, and when I opened to the bookmark there was a special section called "The Great Lakeside High Love Experiment," with pictures of me, Maude, Larry, Wayne, and Dolph; the text was mostly an interview with Maude telling about a talented, funny, and most of all very kind person named Jen Robbins, who had gotten the idea for a love experiment.

Twenty-six

Maude

We met on the beach. It was miles from where the high school kids usually swim. Centuries ago, Jen had taken me there to practice raising my voice and had urged me to shout at the waves.

Jen was standing near the water, resting on her cane. She couldn't see me. I hesitated. Her eyes were toward the tideline. Sand stretched empty as far as you could see. Lots of mist. Flat gray clouds. Cold green waves and tumbling sand and wreckage.

Her clothes seemed dull, her hair listless, uncared for. Behind her, I said, "Hi."

She turned. The scars on her face did not look nice.

"Think it'll rain?" she said softly.

"Maybe."

She took a step forward along the edge of the sea. I followed her. She still had trouble walking.

"Your ankle?"

"It's getting there."

Her eyes seemed empty. The surf was hiss-

181

ing on the gritty sand, broken clam shells tumbling in the undertow.

"Everybody misses you."

"Oh." Her voice was almost dead.

"Jen?"

"What?"

"I don't know what to say to you."

"That's funny," she said with no humor in her voice. "You're usually so good at silence."

Seagulls dropped, flew up in the wind, dropped.

"I wanted to thank you," she said. There was shyness in her voice. I had never heard shyness in Jen.

"You want to thank *me*?" I had trouble getting the words out.

"How is Larry?" she said.

"He wants to see you, Jen. There's a lot to explain."

She stopped and looked directly into my eyes. "Not yet."

Awkwardly, both hands gripping the cane, she lowered herself onto the sand, facing the waves.

"You kept calling every day," she said. Her voice trembled. She dug her hand deep into the sand until the fingers were buried and only her wrist showed. "You sat in the hospital every day."

"I never had a friend, Jen. I didn't want to lose the only one."

She bit her lip and bent her head away from me. Drops of rain touched my face. Overhead the clouds were heavy lead. Way out near the horizon the sky was bright blue.

"You gave me a real life, Jen."

"Did I?" Her chin trembled. "Would you" — she gulped for air — "would you say I'm a good person?"

"You are, Jen."

Her voice broke into sobs, hard sobs. I put my arms around her.

"I want . . . to be . . . happy again," she sobbed. I held her. Then she started laughing and crying at the same time. "It's all so . . . Maude, will you . . . will you tell me . . . I need to hear . . . why you like me."

"Oh, Jen. Of course. There's so much."

I held her hand. I told her why I liked her. We cried and we laughed together.

Twenty-seven

Jen

Sitting with Maude in the back of my father's Oldsmobile — Maude wearing a willowy white dress, me wearing a sleek tomato red sheath and one red silk shoe and one white fiberglass cast — I watched my father bang his horn at a driver who went through a stop sign, my mother puff nervously on her cigarette and show her teeth in a stiff attempt at a smile directed at me, obviously to ease the tension, but the tension was just beginning. I felt like any minute I was going to bail out, tell them to put me in a cab home and let Maude go do the graduating for both of us.

I was biting my lip hard and Maude saw I was sitting on a ton of anxiety and knitted her fingers into mine. "I wish I could make you laugh," she said.

The parking lot at Lakeside High was pretty rough for me, cars on all sides of us disgorging graduates and parents and relatives by the hundreds. I knew people would see me and recognize me and talk about me, and going past them would be like running a gauntlet.

"Maude," I whispered as my father backed the station wagon into a parking spot, "how do you pray, if you're a beginner?"

"I don't know," she said, helping me out of the car. "I just try to ask for what's in my heart."

Putting on our caps and gowns, then walking between the parked cars and newly arriving people, my cane on one side of me, Maude on the other, my parents behind us, people here and there calling hello to me, my stomach practically disintegrated, and my heart pumping so hard I thought I was going to faint. Some of my girl friends loomed up and of course reacted to the scars on my face or tried too hard not to react. The only thing that made it bearable was the grip of Maude's hand around mine.

Even when Miss Passwassel and Coach Bergman were lining up the seniors in the corridor outside the auditorium and you could hear the school orchestra revving up for us to march in, Maude kept her grip on my hand. I was terrified I would trip over my cane or something and on top of it all, I saw Larry and Wayne and Dolph for the first time and they saw me, but, fortunately, before I had to deal with it, Miss Passwassel's eyeballs almost exploded at the sight of Maude holding my hand.

"Maude Harris," Miss Passwassel commanded, "please stop clinging to Jen's hand, and take your place in line like everyone else, *if* you don't mind."

Maude drew herself up to her full height, and looked down amiably at Miss Passwassel. "Sorry, Miss Passwassel, not for anyone."

For a moment I stared in astonishment and admiration at Maude. Then Coach Bergman signaled the two lines of seniors to start the traditional slow step march down the center aisle of the auditorium, where hundreds of faces were turned our way. Maude and I were still holding hands, as if my cane and my scars weren't enough to draw people's eyes toward us. I wanted to run away, but the look on Maude's face was . . . I guess you'd call it radiant, and I suddenly saw how beautiful she was and yet funny too, in a way, if you remembered how she used to be.

All through the graduation ceremony (the singing, the speeches), snapshots kept jumping into my mind — pictures of a shopping cart with Larry and I, the day I came home from Las Vegas, racing down the supermarket aisle and almost knocking Maude over, dowdy scared Maude. I remembered teaching Maude makeup and clothes and how to dance, that night all the knuckles were flying at the Rainy River House, and the warm accepting person-friend I had discovered in Maude.

Now the two of us were together at graduation, and one at a time the seniors were going up to receive their diplomas, but Maude and I went up the steps to the stage arm-in-arm, Maude radiant, me pretty awkward with my cast and cane, and when we took our scrolls tied with gold ribbons the audience burst into a shower of cheers.

Outside in the lobby, after the recessional march, there was hugging, laughing, congratulating. I saw Larry trying to reach me through the hordes of people and he got stuck behind somebody's mother crying on somebody's father's shoulder, so I reached my hand toward him and Larry reached his hand over and squeezed my hand so hard the bones almost cracked.

"Are we *supposed* to feel so mixed up?" Larry said.

Before I could answer him, Wayne and Dolph suddenly had their arms around me and Maude and Larry, squeezing us all together. We all seemed a little embarrassed but happy when we separated, and everybody seemed to have something important to say on the tip of his or her tongue, but before anybody could get a word out, Sonny Goldhammer appeared. He took my hand and led me through the crowd very protectively and out the school doors into the daylight, where his car was parked, the engine humming, a new car, black with yellow flames, looking powerful enough to fly, and Sonny helped me gently into the front seat. My mother and father were watching from the door of the school, a little helplessly and puzzled, but they waved and I think they understood I was doing something that was right for me.

"Why didn't you let me visit you in the hospital?" Sonny said.

"My face," I said.

He took my chin in his hand and moved my face around until he was looking straight at me.

"Scars look rotten," he said roughly.

"Thanks," I said.

"You want me to tell you they look great?"

"No."

"I don't like your scars," he said, "understand? But I like *you*. So let's go celebrate. At a safe speed."

He twisted the key and the engine throbbed and the car smoothed into gear, and my heart going up like a kite, I caught sight of Maude and said, "Please, Sonny, wait!"

Rolling down the window, I saw Maude's face and she seemed not a high school kid anymore but a woman, and she kissed me through the window and said, "I love you, Jen," and I said, "Me too!" Sonny's car eased away from Maude, and she and I began flapping our hands at each other and I saw Larry appear behind Maude and I felt a little stab of pain.

The Great Lakeside High Love Experiment was over. I looked back at the tiny figures on the school lawn as Sonny's car rolled toward the woods on the road to Southhope. It was over, and only the trees and the sky knew what was beginning.